I0589399

All characters in this book are fictional and any resemblance to persons living or dead is purely coincidental.

Copyright © 2016 Destin Douglas

This book is dedicated to my father.

Mist and Timber

Louisa walked directly down the center of the long hallway. She was near six feet tall and wore her shoulder length brown hair straight. The studio was bustling. An actress had overdosed that weekend at a small party in the hills and the publicity department was working overtime to rush her latest movie into theaters.Louisa stopped in front of a large set of wood and copper doors at the end of the hall and quietly placed her ear to the center of the door. She listened for a moment to the muffled sounds of a phone call on the other side.

"I don't really care what state he's in! Get him down to the court house and keep it quiet!" her boss, William Shorter, shouted.

She took a step towards the window and waited for Shorter to finish. Louisa looked out the window and watched a crew of set decorators unload new portions of an Egyptian temple set. Two men struggled to lift a golden sphinx head onto a heavy palette.

The door creaked open, revealing Shorter in

a blue pin stripe banker's vest with sleeves rolled up just under his elbows. He made a small gesture with his hands, his version of an apology, and motioned for Louisa to step inside.

"I've got the head shots for the Bradshaw film." Louisa took a seat and looked up at Will.

William opened the yellow folder and laid the photos out on his desk. Each black and white photograph was of a young actress, all dressed in the same costume.

"I spoke with David. He said they might have found something." Louisa said coolly.

"What do you mean he might have found something?" William asked. "Why haven't I heard about this?"

"I'm telling you now." Louisa reached across the desk and took a cigarette from the gold plated box. She took a lighter from her coat pocket and inhaled deeply as she lit the cigarette.

"It's in some little town up east, a mom and pop sort of a place."

"He'll never go for it."

"Why do you let Bradshaw walk all over you? Tell him to shoot it at one of the spots in the book that we already have. You run the studio, don't you?" She jabbed.

"Things are complicated. Bradshaw doesn't have carte blanche," William dabbed at some of the sweat running down the side of his forehead and opened a window to let out some of the smoke from Louisa's cigarette.

"And neither do you."

Louisa put the cigarette out in a silver ashtray and stood up to leave.

"I was the one that brought this picture in. I need to make this work.""See if you can talk some sense into Bradshaw. Who the hell knows, maybe this is what we've been looking for?" Shorter said.

"Send these photographs back to my office when you're done with them. I need to get more prints made for the costume department." Louisa paused at the door.

"Where are those god damned love birds now?" William asked.

"They've been out there so long I have no idea," Louisa answered.

Louisa thought for a moment, as if trying to remember something, then closed the door behind her.

Her secretary was taking too long to alphabetize some paperwork as Louisa walked past the girl and into her office. She sat down and looked unhappily at the production reports for the Bradshaw film that had become a permanent fixture on the corner of her desk. The thin paperback the film was based on sat lightly on top of the pile.

She picked up the phone and rang for her secretary.

"Get Bradshaw on would you?"

She leaned back in her chair and waiting for the call to connect.

"I'm sorry m'am. Apparently he hasn't been in all week and there is no forwarding number listed. I'm not really sure what else I could do to get a hold of him."

"Thanks Alice."

Louisa clicked the receiver down, noticing out the window a group gathered around the broken remains of the golden sphinx, shattered into thousands of pieces on the hot asphalt.

TWO

Cassie's red blonde hair caught the wind coming in through the open windows. It had already been a long day. Chocolate milkshakes had kept them perked up for the last couple of hours but David felt the exhaustion creeping in. He considered asking Cassie to drive but decided instead to find some place to turn in for the night. They'd see if some small restaurant would still serve them and fall asleep in the strange bed of a strange hotel in some strange county.This was the longest either had worked on a single film, almost two years. Each town exactly like the last. Never quite good enough for the director Bradshaw, back in California. David clenched the wheel a little tighter to stay awake and thought about the snowy hotel they'd searched for all these months. He could almost see it in his mind. Snow covered and set against dark mountains.

"They're still open," Cassie said pointing lazily to one of the small and nameless motels that dotted the western highways.

"Home sweet home!" David said as the hotel door swung open in front of him. He set the two leather suitcases down on the wooden chest of drawers beneath the windows and stretched his back in a large arc. He could have sworn the room was the same as the room in Wichita Falls or Kansas City but had long ago given up trying to prove these strange moments of coincidence. He contented himself with the situation by taking a drink from the small steel flask he kept in the zipper pocket of his garment bag. It had been a long day but they'd made it a couple hundred miles, he thought to himself.

He offered the flask to Cassie, who had removed her earrings and placed them on the short armoire across the room. She walked over and kissed him lightly on the lips. She took the flask and poured a bit of the brown liquor into a glass.Cassie opened the window and lit a cigarette. David lay in bed mostly covered by the thin white sheets, drifting in and out of sleep. She let the smoke thin out and find its way through the window and tapped the ash gently into the white porcelain ashtray on the window sill. She thought about the first time she met David. It was at a release party for one of the first films she had worked on after moving to California. He seemed much younger in her memory of the occasion, a young producer hot off the success of a costumed drama. She wondered how she must have seemed that first night.

He had thought her an actress initially. She had been smart and fiery and opinionated. This had drawn him to her. When he had asked for her number, she had promptly refused. Although every fiber of her body wanted so badly to give in to him. He was smart and funny and sure of himself. She was smarter but still full of wonder and curious about the glamorous town and the people in it.

The cigarette burned down to the paper between her thumb and her forefinger. She smashed it out into the ash tray and looked over at David. Cassie had only had two other boyfriends in the short 27 years she'd been alive. He was difficult at times and being cramped in that small car for weeks on end didn't help. But he was one of the good ones, she thought to herself.

Cassie clicked the small chain that hung from the light on the bedside table and crawled into the warm sheets next to David. She couldn't sleep and wasn't tired but tried to let the warm dark of the hotel room ease over her anyways.

THREE

The top was down on the dark green jaguar as it climbed the hills overlooking downtown. Dark glasses covered Louisa's eyes and her hair was pulled up in a tight bun at the back of her head. She wore white leather driving gloves and shifted the car into a lower gear as she rounded a corner and came to a steeper incline. She liked driving, she always had. The car was the first thing she had purchased after being promoted to work under Shorter at the studio. Her mother would have considered the car opulent.Bradshaw's house was in the deep canyons far from the parties and commotion in Los Angeles. He was notorious for receiving no guests and Louisa had been trying to set up this meeting for days at this point. One of his interchangeable assistants suggested she wait until he returned to work at the studio lot to see him. He didn't like to be bothered at his house, the assistant had apologetically insisted to Louisa over the phone. Even if she was one of Worldwide Picture's newest executives, it was time Bradshaw started to take her a bit more seriously.

The road flattened out into a long straightaway. Louisa kicked the large car into a higher gear and twisted the stretched leather around the steering wheel. She'd dealt with difficult people before and knew that this time wasn't any different.

She didn't think Bradshaw was blowing her off because she was a woman, all in all he seemed fairly receptive to the idea of working under a woman and showed everyone a quite similar amount of disregard. He was probably queer, she mused to herself. At least that would explain why he hadn't made a pass at her at some point during the two, going on three, pictures they had done together. The car ate pavement hungrily as it sped towards the strange mansion in the lost hills. The city fell away behind Louisa.

She parked in front of the large iron gate that shuttered the house off from the rest of the street and pressed the buzzer. For a few moments nothing happened. She was afraid briefly that she had been wrong and the director truly was away from Los Angeles. She would feel foolish for making such a long drive for nothing.

"Come up," the speaker buzzed in Bradshaw's deep voice.

The iron gate slid backwards into the foliage and Louisa pulled the car slowly onto the grounds. The driveway was most of a mile long and would have had its own street name in the small town in Arkansas where Louisa had grown up. She was both disgusted with and jealous of the success of the man that had built them. She knew she would never have anything so rare and extravagant for herself.The drive came to a large circle in front of the house. Louisa parked the car and took off her driving gloves before getting out of the car. She took off the red sunglasses and hung them from the deep neck of her button down blouse. She stood for a moment and took in the majesty of the house.

It was a combination of wood and brick designed to blend in with and accentuate the surrounding forest. The house's long, sharp lines cut into the cliffs at the building's back. The massive walls of clear glass gave the whole structure a sense of being only partially there.

"I could live in a place like this," Louisa said to herself.

She opened the front door without knocking. It was unlocked and the large, solid wood door came back lightly on its oiled hinges.

"Hello?" Louisa said.

"Over here. In the back." Bradshaw's deep voice sounded from a distant corner of the house.

Louisa made her way through a glossy marbled kitchen, eventually finding herself in a small room attached the southernmost part of the building. Unlike the rest of the house, it was small and crowded with books and tools. Bradshaw was there, bent over what looked like a large metal arm composed of long struts, springs, and steel cables. He hardly looked up when she entered the room.

He was a large man, just short of fat, with a mane of long black hair that tangled into a matted mess around his circular face. His eyes were deep set with dark brown irises that just barely stood out against the black circles that framed them, giving him a sense of emotionless intelligence. He wore a white linen shirt rolled up to his elbows that was covered in grease. He struggled to pull a steel cable through the slotted groove of a pulley. Satisfied the cable was in place and bolted down, he turned to Louisa with his kindest smile.

"What does it do?" She asked.

"It opens up a whole new world for us."

"Sounds exciting, you going to be able to put it back together?" She asked, sitting in one of the light wicker chairs.

The room was covered with photographic equipment in various levels of disrepair. Shining pieces of glass and small parts of various lenses sat on the leather surface of the desk, laid out like pieces of a soon to rise monster in a dim laboratory. She picked one up and looked through the curved surface of the lens towards the strange man. His figure was distorted and nearly monstrous through the lens. He took the glass gently from her hands and wiped the edges she had touched with a soft cloth.

"It's a pleasure to see you Louisa, but you don't tend to drive up to the canyon for social calls. Is there anything that I can help you with on this fine day?" Bradshaw asked.

"Actually yes. Shorter and the money people

back in New York are getting a little restless." She said.

"They're always restless. That's why they're in charge of the money." He said calmly.

"Still, this is shaping into something a little different from what they're used to."

"It is different. That's why they're restless."

"Be that as it may. I'm here to get a sense of where your head's at and to see if we can find some sort of middle ground."

"I liked the head shots Shorter sent over last week. I'm sure both would do nicely if you're here to force my hand."

"I don't care about the fucking bit parts, I'm here about the hotel," she said.

Bradshaw poured himself a small glass of expensive whiskey and offered it to Louisa. She politely refused. She didn't drink much anymore and didn't want to give Bradshaw an advantage.

"If there is no hotel there is no film. It's as simple as that." She said in her coolest voice.

"There will be a film. I assure you."

"If you have another thirty million dollars lined up I'd appreciate it if you would let us know back at the office. I'm sure it would ease some of the tension on the lot."

"You've got some of your best people on it. That's what you told me yourself." Bradshaw said.

"And they've been looking around the world for more than two years now." Bradshaw turned back to working on the strange metal contraption that filled most of the room.

"It just won't do. I'm afraid you may not understand."

"Well, please enlighten me," Louisa leaned forwards in her chair.

"The hotel is the heart of the film. With no hotel, we've got no heart. A person can't live without a heart. I'm sure you can see that."

"It's called movie magic Bradshaw. The silver screen. You can't come up with some way to shortcut this so we could fit the film into this year's production slate? Why won't you just let me help you?"

"I'm afraid it's just not that easy." he said with a small shake of his head.

FOUR

The cold air started to turn to snow as the red Plymouth rushed south. It was the first moments of winter and Cassie cursed the small car's heaters. They were 160 miles north of New York City. David had called ahead to a friend of his who graciously offered to put them up for a day or two. The friend's name had been Clyde Herbert but he'd changed it for show business. He and David had served in the signal corps together in Korea. Clyde was an up and coming actor who, for the last few years, had played mostly supporting parts of caring fathers or ex-cons in television commercials. But David's friend's luck had changed recently. Clyde was up for a lead man role in one of the new pilots shooting that spring. Cassie didn't particularly care for Clyde but his wife Edith was nice enough, and Cassie looked forward to a brief vacation from their tedious work.

As the miles rushed by, the great looming structure of the city became visible across the bridge. Cassie had spent a few weeks in New York as a tourist in her youth. She had found the great bustle of city attractive but could never fully understand the appeal it held for the millions of young creatives and ambitious businessmen that flocked to its marble and pavement each year.

She could never quite see herself living in a place without a sky.

"Clyde said they just moved into a wonderful old building. Wrought iron gargoyles, great marble facades that line the entrance ways. They even have a bellboy. How wild is that?" David said.

"Isn't he still playing mostly bit parts?" Cassie asked."Just living up there has opened up a whole new world of contacts and it sounds like things are really turning around for him. You know that he and Edith had been having a tough time of it for a while now?"

"Last I'd heard they were coming back from their honeymoon and quite content." Cassie said.

"Edith miscarried a few months ago. She's fine and the doctors say she will be right as rain in a few months. I just wanted you to know, in case it comes up."

"That poor thing." Cassie said.

She turned her head out the window to watch the colorful city rush by. She wasn't willing to have the same argument they'd had so many times before. She couldn't force David to have a child. He would come around when he was ready, she thought to herself. Maybe Edith and Clyde would rub off on David a little while they were in New York. Neither of them lived a life that would be easy or comfortable with a child but the thought of it still brought a smile to her face.

David steered the car off the large expressway

and they found themselves somewhere in Manhattan. The traffic was almost unbearable and the snow coming down didn't make things any better. The wheels skidded for a brief moment as David turned down the west side of Central Park, but he managed to get control just before the car slid into another lane. They suffered the curses, shouts, and car horns and were quickly on their way again.

"He said it was on 72nd," David said as he leaned forwards against the seatbelt trying to read the green and white letters of the street signs as they zipped south on the busy road.

"I think that's it," she said just as they passed the street.

David let out a good natured laugh as he drive by 72nd, "I guess we get do a little sight seeing." "That must be it," She said pointing to large green spires that stretched up from the building, standing sharply apart from the glass and steel superstructures that had sprung up around the ancient building.

The Dakota stood like a lone flag of some time long gone and lost to the world around it. Part gothic cathedral, part Swiss chalet, with a dash of Madison avenue elegance thrown in for good measure, the apartment building forced one to admire its elegance. As the car pulled closer, Cassie noticed the small crowd gathering on the street in front of the apartment complex.

A siren shrieked loudly and an ambulance rushed past their small red car towards the scene.

"There must have been some sort of accident." Cassie said as she covered her mouth with her hand.

David parked the car on the far end of the block and they cautiously moved towards the crowd on the sidewalk.

"David!" a small voice cried.

It was Edith. As she parted from the crowd towards them, Cassie found herself jealous of the woman. She was shorter than Cassie, with a petite hourglass figure that seemed more like an artist's charcoal sketch of a woman than any person Cassie had met. Her hair was tight against the back of her head in an arcing bob. Her eyes were large in comparison to her small face, giving her a quality of both beauty and gravitas.

"It's awful what's happened." Edith said, just short of tears. She embraced David and Cassie with a quick hug and turned to look back at the scene a few yards away on the street. "She's dead. She jumped. A girl from the building." Edith replied.

"That's terrible," Cassie said.

Through the crowd of onlookers, Cassie could just make out the white sheet laid on the sidewalk. Small patches of crimson bled through the fabric as white flakes of snow began to fall. A police man scribbled a few notes into a blue notebook, interviewing an older couple.

"Did you know her?" Cassie asked.

"Her name was Lucy, I don't know that I ever knew her last name. She lived in one of the flats above us. She seemed like a nice girl. I can't believe anyone would do something like this to themselves." Edith said in a frail voice.

Two men in white medical coats collected the body on a metal gurney. Cassie looked on with a small feeling of guilt, unable to take her eyes away. She saw the girl's pail white wrist beneath the sheet. Cassie watched as a few thin flakes of snow fell into the scarlet stains on the pavement and melted.

"Well, welcome to New York," Edith said with a failed but courteous posture.

"Thank you so much for having us," Cassie said.

"Do you have any luggage? I can have one of the valets bring it up if you'd like."

"Oh no need, we travel light. You have no idea how good it will feel to be in place where people actually live instead of just hotel room after hotel room," David said.

"Let me show you the apartment. Clyde is out at an audition but he should be home in no time."

"That sounds just fine," Cassie said with a reassuring smile.

The men loaded the ambulance and pulled out onto the street. Cassie watched as the scene slowly became empty, everyone returning to the day's work and chores that occupied their minds and time before the strange death of a strange woman.

She turned to see that Edith and David had already started for the great entrance of the apartment building and rushed to follow them through the great copper and glass doors just before they closed behind her.

The Dakota's interior was majestic, black and white marble tile laid out in octagonal designs stretching from wall to wall. The large concierge desk was a deep and old hard wood, stained from years of work and use. It's front carved into a series of beautiful half pearls and top edge rimmed with a dark ivory. The two men working behind the desk were well dressed in matching black wool suites. One of them wore a smart mustache and gold pocket watch chained across the double breasted vest of his suite. The other was older and his white hair stood out against the warm tones of the room and the black wool of his clothes.

"Good Evening." The younger man said and tipped his hat to Edith and Cassie as they passed the front desk towards the large elevator.

The intricate iron door slid into place behind them as they boarded the large elevator. The man running the lift greeted Edith warmly. He pushed the handle forward and the cage jumped with a start into the higher parts of the old building. Cassie watched with curiosity as the inner working of the building fell past them. The wires hummed with the weight of the carriage and Edith smiled as the copper bell rung with a soft chime. They had reached the 8th floor.

The bellman slid the great door back into itself and David thanked him as they exited. It was the top floor of the large building, and was split into two large wings that extended over the large L shape of the building's footprint. They followed the thick golden stripe running down the deep purple carpet around a corner and finally came to an apartment.

"We're still moving in really, so please don't take any notice of the mess," Edith said in her soft voice.

"I'm sure the place looks fantastic." David said.

The large door swung into the apartment and revealed a large and comfortable home. It was spacious but not gaudy, well built but not opulent. Dark hard wood floors ran throughout the apartment. The dining room had a large set of floor to ceiling windows that looked out onto the forested park corralled amidst concrete towers.

Boxes and various furniture sat wrapped in thick plastic sheeting all around. Some of the windows were open and a slight breeze came in to fight the oppressive heat of hissing radiators scattered through the apartment. Soft snow danced outside and hung in the curling air like lines of cursive. For all the beauty of the place, Cassie couldn't help but notice a slight odor somewhere between rust and charred ash.

"You two must be tired after that drive. Can I offer either of you something to drink? We just moved in but we've got a pretty full bar hiding around here somewhere," Edith said as she steered the group towards the kitchen.

As they passed through the long hallway leading through the center of the apartment Cassie paused to look through a partially opened door into one of the bedrooms of the house. In the center of the room a painter's tarp was pulled into a cluttered ball, next to it two buckets of paint sat with pale blue streaks dried on their sides. The wall with the glass windows was painted a pale, almost grey, blue. Small portions of the corner showed the white primer coat where the painter hadn't finished. The other wall was covered in old peeling wallpaper with purple flowers fading against a white and blue checkered print.

David sipped the cocktail and envied his friend Clyde's large apartment and small beautiful wife. He was a happy man and he hated New York, but still he couldn't help himself. Cassie made a joke that got Edith laughing quietly. David pretended to laugh even though he hadn't heard the story.

"Clyde says you're working on some big picture, can't hardly even talk about it," Edith said.

"It's not so big as that." Cassie replied.

"That must be so wild. I get what I can out of Clyde when he gets home each night, but those are mostly just television commercials. No real movie stars or anything but he likes to pretend."

"Well this one may not have any stars either if we can't find a place to shoot the damn thing," Cassie said as she finished her cocktail.

"Do you have any leads? Any good places in the running? Maybe you could shoot here? It would certainly liven the place up a little. I think the average age in the building is just under 150 years old," Edith said with a devilish smile.

"Thanks for the offer but it wouldn't work. We've been on the hunt for almost two years now and nothing has worked for this man. Part of me thinks we're never to make this film."

David turned to watch the city rush around outside the window and wondered if the snow had covered all the blood on the pavement below.

"What sort of place are you looking for?" Edith asked.

"A grand old hotel. Something majestic and haunted. It's for a horror picture," David said still looking out the window.

"That's so exciting. I wish I got to travel and see things and hunt out the setting of a big Hollywood movie!" Edith said as she refilled everyone's glasses.

"It's not quite as grand as you might think.

This is the first time we haven't stayed in a hotel in months. I used to think that diner food was my favorite food but I'd be happy if I didn't have to eat at another drive through my whole life," David said.

"It's not as bad as he makes it out to be. It's just a different sort of life. Living out of suitcases and staying in a different town every night. It really means a lot to us, you and Clyde for letting us stay here a few days," Cassie said.

"Stay here as long as you want. To be honest it gets a little lonesome in this apartment."

She hadn't known Edith well before this moment but she couldn't help feeling sorry for the poor girl. In the right light she might have looked beautiful but here she seemed more like a child lost in a swirling crowd.With a loud crash, the front door opened and closed.

"Baby, sweet baby I sure am home!" Clyde yelled from the end of the long hallway.

Clyde stopped in the kitchen door frame. A large grin stretched from ear to ear. Tall with trim dark hair and a muscular build, he wore a well tailored suit that fit him like a sheet of aluminum wrapped around a fighter plane.

"Davey boy!" Clyde shouted.

Clyde opened his arms and embraced David with all his strength. Then he turned to Cassie with the same enthusiasm. She gave in and hugged him back, her arms not quite reaching all the way around the large man. Clyde turned to his beautiful bride and twirled her gracefully with one hand high in the air, bringing her back around and dipped her low and carefully by the small of her back. He planted a large, over acted kiss on her bright red lips.

"I don't know about any of you, but I'm starving." Clyde said.

Clyde and Edith lent David and Cassie heavier coats and they all left the building to find dinner. The snow had mostly stopped but it was colder now and fast wind came down the streets. Cassie pulled Edith's huge scarf up around her neck as they headed towards the broad street running alongside the park.

They settled for small Italian place that seemed quiet enough with a name Cassie could hardly pronounce. They sat at a small table in the back of the restaurant. Clyde ordered a large bottle of wine for the table.

"Can't find stuff like this in Los Angles, can you buddy boy?" Clyde asked as the first portions were brought out.

The food was incredible and there wasn't anything like this in California. But it almost seemed like cheating as Cassie watched the old Italian women work over the hot stove tops a few feet behind them. Great heaping portions of pasta and bread came out, one after another and Cassie thought for a moment that she was going to pop.

Tray after tray, Clyde kept ordering, bracing each new dish with another bottle of wine he swore was the only thing that could accompany such fine food.

Clyde seemed like he was built of silver springs coiled tight. The conversation was quick and superfluous. Cassie had met Clyde when he lived in California before he had married Edith. He'd had a few flings with some of her girlfriends and it had soured her to the notion of Clyde Herbert but he seemed a different man now. More sure of himself, full of bright ideas and ten cent words that drifted lightly across the table. She couldn't help but find herself laughing along with everyone else as he spoke about an assistant director that been caught in a very awkward moment of embrace with a young man that worked in the costume department of Clyde's new television show. Cassie nearly spilled one of the large glasses of the strong red wine into her lap as she laughed.

Clyde's energy and laughter seemed infectious and Cassie noticed David laughing and making everyone laugh in turn. It was one of the things she admired about him.

The only one left out was Edith. She laughed lightly at the old stories and strange tales but it was clear to Cassie she was putting on an act. She laughed at each brief opening in conversation like a gymnast working a well rehearsed routine. Cassie couldn't tell if Clyde knew or not.

Two hours later they were the only people left in the restaurant and most of the staff had gone home. A young hostess and a thirty something maître de with a thin black mustache flirted at the front of the restaurant and brought another bottle of wine every time Clyde waved his hand above his head. The party showed no sign of slowing down. And then, Cassie noticed the small drop of blood appear at the base Edith's nose.

"Edith, you're... you're bleeding," Cassie said.

Cassie offered her napkin to the girl. Edith dabbed gently at her nose for a moment, then rushed to the bathroom. A cold silence hung over the table in the space that was filled stories of good times gone by just moments before.

Edith stood in front of the mirror holding the thick white napkin to the front of her face. The napkin almost all red and the blood didn't seem to stopping.

"You poor thing. Is there anything I can do?" Cassie said.

"No. I'll be fine." Edith said, her voice muffled.

"It's really nothing, every once in a while this sort of thing happens," Edith said softly. She turned to face the mirror and was gently dabbing at the trickle of blood running down her chin and down the side of her neck. The door creaked open and Clyde stood framed in the doorway by the bright kitchen lights.

"Edith? Are you alright?" He asked.

"I'm fine, it must have been the wine," She said. "I'm more embarrassed than anything else."

"Nonsense!" Cassie said, dabbing some of the dried blood off the girl's neck."I think I'm ready to go home now," she said forcing a half smile. Clyde pulled a large wad of green bills from his overcoat pocket and left a large tip on the table. David pulled the thick wool coat up around his ears and walked outside to hail on of the yellow cabs zipping by outside.

"1912 West 72nd please," Clyde told the cab driver as they all piled in.

The old driver put the car in gear and they zoomed across one of the large avenues. David paid for the cab as Clyde and Cassie helped Edith into the lobby of the apartment building.

In the lobby, David was surprised to find an elderly couple dressed as if returning from an extravagant and severe party swarming Edith as she struggled to hide her fatigue and keep the polite smile on her face.

"Let Phillip have a look at it my dear. He was a doctor in the war," the old, small lady cawed.

"It's true dear Edith, I was staff surgeon at the field hospital in Merrimount, saved nearly a thousand lives. I'd hope I could take care of a little nosebleed," The man said with a strange, slightly European accent.

David looked curiously towards Cassie while

Clyde visited quietly with the old man.

"Nan and Phillip these are some of my oldest friends. Meet David and Cassie," Clyde said.

The couples exchanged introductions quickly before Cassie excused herself and Edith.

"Of course, of course." Phillip said in his strange voice.

"We've got to be going anyway. We're going to see one of those fine pianists in from Italy for the winter. I'll tell you all about it my dears," Nan said with a warm, motherly smile.

"Please do. You two take care of yourselves out there tonight. The roads might as well be paved with ice," Clyde said with his hundred dollar smile.

Soon, they were in the elevator shooting towards the apartment.

"Those are the Blackerts, our neighbors on the west wing. They've been all sorts of help since we moved in. I've been so caught up with work these past few months. They're practically part of the family." Clyde said, looking up to watch the open air shaft of the elevator rushing past them.

"They don't have any children of their own so I guess it makes sense they'd take a shine to Edith here," Clyde continued.

Cassie looked over at Edith. The girl seemed happy to be rid of the old couple and looked up only when the elevator chime signaled they were on the eighth floor. They walked the rest of the way down the long hallway without speaking.The two couples said good night to each other and went to their separate rooms. Edith had already worked up the guest room with spare linens and David and Cassie were glad to finally find themselves alone for a moment. The room had the same strange smell as the rest of the house but neither David nor Cassie minded after all those long months in hotel rooms and Cassie took a certain joy in hanging her clothes up in the closet. David laid back in the bed, happy to have made it New York in one piece.

That night was the coldest night of the year. It didn't snow anymore but the pipes in the old building creaked and moaned as they fought off the urge to burst in the walls. The windows kept the night out and David held Cassie close in the small bed. The sun came up and drifted in through the sheer window curtains.

Cassie awoke trying to remember the details of a strange dream like a sailor grasping for the last rope as he falls towards the black sea beneath the shining hull of a vessel too large to turn back.

David was already up and pulling one of his large turtleneck sweaters over his head. His hair was a mess of blonde curls that came up at sharp, random angles. Cassie couldn't help but laugh.

"Morning sunshine. How'd you sleep?" David asked.

"I'm not sure," she said as she stretched out

in the bed.

Edith sat at the small coffee table under the window in the kitchen wrapped in a red and white silk robe and sipped steaming coffee from a blue cup. She greeted David and Cassie with a smile and poured two cups of coffee. "I'm glad your heat is working. It must be damn close to zero out there," David said as he gulped down the warm black liquid.

Clyde burst into the kitchen struggling with the knot of a colorful, checkered tie. He leaned down to kiss his wife on the top of her head then turned to greet Cassie and David.

"Good morning you two love birds. Drink up, Edith makes a mean pot of coffee, it'll keep you warm through the freeze."

"Are you feeling any better Edith?" Cassie asked.

Clyde poured a cup of coffee for himself. Edith brushed the loose strands of her thin hair up around her ear. She looked a little more pale than yesterday.

"Oh, I'm fine, just embarrassed to have ruined such a fine evening. Let's just pretend it never happened."

"As long as your alright," Cassie said, taking the woman's small hands in her own.

"Listen, I've got to take off. Big audition today. But I ran into the Blackerts last night after you all had gone to bed."

"You went out last night?" Edith asked, surprised.

"I ran out for smokes and ran into them in the elevator. They were just getting home from that piano concert. They were worried sick about you," Clyde said, shoulders raised just slightly, as if in defense.

"What a thoughtful pair," Edith said flatly.

"Do you two know many others in the building?" Cassie asked.

"Pretty much just them. Even that Edith seems to think is a bit much. She says we shouldn't encourage them to butt into our business."

"I think they're perfectly kind people, I'd just like to have a few more friends our own age. We're already living in a building that's practically a mausoleum."

"She loves the place. She really does, I swear," Clyde joked across the kitchen table.

"They were worried sick about you Edith. With all the medical issues we've been going through the last couple of months and everything. They just want you to be happy and healthy. They invited us out to the opera tonight. Had some extra tickets I suppose. Said the two of you should come along. So? What do you all say?" Clyde asked.

"That really is very sweet of them. But I don't want David and Cassie to feel like they have to go entertain a crazy old couple from our building. They're only in town for the day."

"We'd love to go with you." David said. "We'll have the day to do a little sight seeing and be back in time for the show. Seems like it a fine thing to do in the city."

"Great, I'll phone down and tell them. The show starts at eight so that should leave you guys plenty of time to see whatever y'all want to see and I'll be all done with the audition by then. It's gonna be a swell night. You two just wait and see." Clyde said.

With a small flip of the wrist he pulled the tie tight down around itself. It fell just where he wanted.

"Wish me luck everyone. This is the big one," he kissed Edith again on the top of the head and rushed out the door.

Edith was glad she would have a little company today, unlike so many days in the large empty apartment that echoed of a life they may never fully create.

"Break a leg honey," She sad said mostly to herself as she watched her husband walk away and heard the door close.

"You sure did marry a wild one," David said to Edith with a laugh.

They sat at the breakfast table eating toast spread thin with raspberry jam as they decided what to do with the cold day. There was plenty of time before the show and neither Cassie nor David wanted to waste the day.

FIVE

William Shorter had been the head of Worldwide pictures for 12 years before he ran into any real trouble. His father ran the studio before him, teaching his son the intricacies of the motion picture business and leaving William qualified and capable. William Shorter took his job seriously. He was proud of what he did and the skill with which he did it. That only made it that much harder to know he would fail.

Shorter liked Bradshaw. They had been young stars together years ago, reinventing the way things were done in the glitzy picture town. When first they met, each was young and hungry and just smart enough to pull it all off. Now Shorter just hoped his friendship would not undo him.

The picture had been at a complete standstill for almost 18 months. The large machine of the industry had begun turning its precise wheels, gearing up for principle photography and now William Shorter was fully aware that he was out of options.

The mistake had happened quickly and quietly. He knew he should just admit what he had done and be rid of the whole mess. Bradshaw had made threats even paid, proven and prolific old timers couldn't get themselves out from under and it had cost him. That was just they the way that it went here. Sometimes you got lucky. Some times you went bust. William Shorter knew he was no longer lucky, but he would be god damned before he was the one getting hurt.

It was almost funny how little it had taken to undo him, Shorter thought to himself as he halfheartedly cleaned his desk. In the motion picture business every film ran up and down. A department tabulated the cost and printed out long reports that presented the film's cost and projected profits in a tidy manila folder. Then the studio heads would signal yes or no like Roman emperors paying out judgment. Five thousand dollars, that was all. Just 5 thousand dollars pulled from another picture Worldwide was putting out and siphoned into Bradshaw's latest picture to keep the ball rolling for an old friend. Who wouldn't have done the same thing for someone they'd known for the better part of 25 years. Who wouldn't have done the same thing when you thought about how much money the director's last four films had made. William Shorter had simply taken the risk, knowing full and well the value of the chips he stacked. He'd taken the chance just like he knew his father would have done. Just like he knew he was meant to. Bradshaw hadn't returned Shorter's phone calls for most of the month. It wasn't that they were close friends but Shorter expected a bit more of a response as the head of the studio and man that had put everything on the line for an old friend. Still, there was nothing.

When the call came, it came as a surprise. Bradshaw asked to meet at a small bar up in San Berdeee where the interstate stopped at the cliffs north of town. Shorter shuffled the papers that filled his desk, clearances and permissions from one of the westerns shooting on the studio's backlots as part of a new program letting independent producers onto the lots. They were trying to rent out the space when they weren't shooting to keep the wheels on the machine running at all times. Shorter wasn't sure if it was worth it. There had already been two injured technicians and the insurance got a lot more complicated when the producer wasn't tied to the studio in some way.

Shorter didn't like the way the town was changing. He wondered how his father would fit into this new world with its hot lights running all day and the studio making more movies than anyone could ever hope to craft with even a degree of skill or cunning. Maybe it was best the old man wasn't around to see his son in the big chair at the back of the studio.

Shorter stayed later than his secretary. He always did. Partly because he worked more than anyone else on the lot and partly because he liked the peace and quiet of the building after everyone left. Those moments late in the evening when the lot was finally silent was Shorter's favorite part of the day and he would sometimes stay and work throughout the night without even noticing.

No one else was around to hear the call or they might had have thought it strange. Bradshaw apologized for his forgetfulness and asked to meet to discuss the project. He told Shorter he had some real exciting news, something that was going to make everything all right and get both of them back up to the top of the heap. Shorter didn't have the heart to tell his friend over the phone it was all over. He feigned interested and agreed to meet at the little bar at the end of the expressway.

William Shorter ran the fictitious numbers of the film through his head. The first five thousand had gone quickly. Then it was 15 thousand. Before Shorter could right his wrong or pull the plug on the account altogether, the picture was almost 2 million down on the books. Shorter knew that was a number you couldn't come back from and you couldn't keep the secret forever. He'd known it was all over for months but he tried to keep the act up for as long as he could in the strange hopes that the one time boy wonder could pull something incredible out of the wreckage.The parking lot was filled with warm orange lights that stretched around the lot. The bar was nicer than he had expected. Thick grey rope and assorted sailing accessories hung throughout the building and the place seemed to wish it was something else. Shorter didn't mind much and ordered a drink he'd never heard of before.

Two empty glasses in front of him, Bradshaw sat at the end of the bar watching a partially talented guitarist on the dim stage in the back of the old room. White light circled the boy on the stool as he forgot more notes than he remembered. He limped through the rest of the song and the bar clapped three or four times for him as he walked to the back of the place and off into the real dark behind the stage.

"How goes it?" Shorter asked.

"'Bout just like always," Bradshaw answered. "I want to apologize for the last couple of weeks. I haven't really been myself. A lot has changed, I feel liked I owe you an apology in person. Sorry. Sorry and thanks."

"It's alright," Shorter answered.

"I know about the money. I went through the books myself."

"Well you're the first to find out. You can turn me in if you want."

"I wanted to thank you."

"Don't. It's over, it's all over. It's all so fucked, even if we started shooting tomorrow, we couldn't make it through the end of the week. The money's gone. The studio is pulling the project out of the pipeline and there isn't anything I can do about it, even if I wanted to."

"That's understandable."

"Fuck off. Don't bring this shit full circle in

the last hour. You've been driving this picture into the ground ever since you got it in your head that you wanted to turn this god forsaken book into a Saturday night special. You are the single worst thing that has ever happened to me," Shorter said, his eyes tired.

Shorter felt guilty as soon as the sharp words left his mouth and waived the bartender with the rolled up sleeves over. He asked for two beers and two gins with seltzer. The kid turned and got to work on the cocktails and William Shorter turned to apologize to his old friend.

"You're right to say that, you really are. I've been ruining that picture for most of a year now. I see that now," Bradshaw said. "But I worked it out. All the way through. A lot has changed in the last couple of weeks Will. I don't think you understand just how big of a beast we're dealing with here."

"That doesn't mean it's not over friend. The well dried up and there isn't anything left. You've gotta understand that. I'm hanging on for my life here. I wasn't even called in to last month's board meeting. You know what that means?"

Bradshaw sat silent.

"You took your fucking time and you ruined us both."

His beer was empty and Shorter turned to the cold gin glass. Bradshaw had given him this talk half a dozen times when one of their projects looked like it was going to go stillborn in the water. Each time Shorter agreed to press forward and move their pawns that much further down the board. Each time Bradshaw proved himself a competent and worthy partner, following through on his promises and eventually bringing in another victory at the far end of each fighting field.

"Just one more drink. I can make you see the way this will work." Bradshaw pleaded.

"Maybe you're just too fucking smart to realize, but when the money stops coming in next week, you'll get the picture."

"Neither of us are doing it for the money."

William Shorter ordered two more of the gin drinks from the bar and held his head as he waited for the boy behind the bar to bring them over.

"It's not about the money. You're right. But you've damn near ruined me and if I can't bring some sort of return back to the old men reading the numbers off the thin lines in those board rooms the game is over and they take away everything. Everything I've worked towards. Everything my father worked towards. Everything I could ever give to my kid some day. Do you have any idea what that feels like? Did you even stop to consider for one second what I've done for you and how far out I am on this?"

"Don't walk away from this William. It can work. I can make it work," Bradshaw said.

"It's a damn fool thing to follow you any

further. It was good knowing you and I still count you as a friend but you can go fuck yourself," Shorter said as he raised a glass and put the last of his gin down.

Bradshaw did the same and coughed slightly as the white hot liquid rushed down his throat.

"I'm asking you not to walk out that door," Bradshaw said after the boy brought over the bill and Shorter paid.

"You don't understand, I never even came in that door."

Shorter turned over the engine to his car happy to be done with the strange man. He felt lighter in his shoulders somehow and could feel the gin working on his mind. He put the car in gear and pulled out of the yellow lit parking lot into the dark stretch of road that peeled down the coast back towards Los Angeles.

SIX

The office was forwarding all of Shorter's calls to Louisa's office because he never showed up for work that morning. She had hardly even had a chance to tend to the work that piled up on her desk because she was doing so much of William Shorter's business. Two of the financial officers from New York had called that morning and Louisa was starting to think there was some sort of plan in the works to make her life a living hell.

The door bell to her office rung and for a moment Louisa considered pretending to have already left for the day. She knew it wouldn't work and picked up the phone.

"Hello, come on in," she said.

It was the mousy girl that worked near the phones in the front of the floor. Louisa couldn't remember her name.

"Ms. McKay. It's someone from New York. He says his name is David. It's a collect call. Do you want to put him through?" the girl asked in her small voice.

"Sure, I'll take him on two," Louisa answered.

She picked up the phone receiver and clicked the line over.

"Hey there, what gives?" she asked into the

phone.

"Just calling to check in. We're in New York, leaving tomorrow. Wanted to see if there were any updates."

"Nothing new on this end."

"How's the office?" David asked.

"Still Sunny. Just like it always."

Silence hung on the line. Louisa wondered what David was thinking.

"Shorter hasn't come in today, I'm picking up all the slack and it's starting to be my own personal nightmare. My phone won't stop ringing, you're not helping unless you've got some good news for me."

"Sounds like I should let you get back to work."

"How's that sweet faced little girl treating you?", Louisa asked, her voice raising just slightly in tone.

"Be nice."

"I like to pretend. That's why I work in Hollywood," Louisa said coolly.

"She's great, thanks for asking. We're in New York. Going to a fancy opera later, got invited by an old couple that lives in the same building as an old buddy from my more courageous days."

"You're still brave David. Well, you could be if you wanted."

"Take care, I'll call soon if I've got anything to call about." David said.

"You should call anyways."

"Take care Louisa."

Louisa clicked the phone back down onto its black vinyl saddle and leaned back in the large chair behind the mahogany desk for a moment.

She'd almost loved David once, a few years ago. She hadn't understood what it was about him she enjoyed when they were a couple. He wasn't as smart of most of the men she dated and he came from a middle class, almost painfully average background. But she liked him anyways and that was good enough at the time. There was something about him that gave the impression of trustworthiness without the carelessness. In a way, she was glad he had been the one to end it, for Louisa had always known secretly she would never have had the strength to leave him.

Sometimes she thought about what would have been if David had stuck around. She didn't think about it too long. She never did.

A soft rap on the thick door filled the office and shook Louisa out of her own head.

"Come in," she said, just a bit more exasperated than before. The girl was holding a pile of teletypes folded into half a dozen thick manila envelopes.

"These are just in from accounting. They need you to take a look at them."

"That's Shorter's business, I've got work to do here."

"They told me to tell you that Mr. Shorter

hasn't been in the office since last Friday. I just print out the documents and deliver them, sorry Ms. McKay."

"Leave them on the desk," Louisa said.

The girl did as she was told and closed the door behind her. Louisa opened the thick folder and started working her way through the file. She could hardly make heads or tails of the financial statements. Numbers referenced back onto themselves and accounts mixed and matched from their first entries. Louisa had never seen a successful company present such a tidy and organized face to the world yet run so erratically in its accounts.

She buzzed the girl outside for another cup of coffee and settled down to work through the papers.

The blacktop of the lot was hotter than usual for this time of year. Louisa made her way across it like a Greek goddess, heels clicking furiously against the pavement towards Will Shorter's office. This was going to stop one way or the other, there wasn't any real way that she was going to pick up for the man, not when she had so much work of her own.

Shorter's assistant could hardly keep up with the piles of paper being dropped off at her desk. Louisa almost felt sorry for her. She struggled to put the phone down as Louisa pushed her way through the large oak doors into the office.

"Ms. McKay, I'm sorry he hasn't come in all day. You're not the first person to come looking for him." The girl said.Louisa didn't respond.

The room was empty. One of the windows was open and a slight breeze had blown some of the yellow loose-leaf papers onto the floor. Louisa bent to pick the paper up and put it back in a neat stack on the desk before turning to close the window.

"Shorter, you son of a bitch. I don't know where you are but I'll kill you if you ever show up," Louisa said to herself.She sat down in the overstuffed chair behind the desk and spun around slowly in a large circle. She envied this desk. She envied everything about William Shorter's life. He was the modern day equivalent to the royal families of Europe and no matter what might happen Louisa would never reach his inherited success. She was a brilliant, beautiful woman who worked hard and was unafraid of the world of show business. She'd done well for herself thus far, and there was no reason to think her luck was going to run out any time soon.

She stared up at the ceiling and decided to give herself another five minutes alone in the quiet office. It was better than going back to the shit storm that had descended on her small corner of the world. Two of the films under her care were already over budget and the picture shooting in Italy was having problems getting the camera equipment through customs. One of the local fixers had put a second mortgage on his home to get the gear in through the border and it didn't seem like it was going to be possible to get the rest of the film stock to the location in time for the shoot. She made a mental note to give the man that had put up his house some sort of Christmas bonus. An endless amount of shit was coming in though the front door over the next couple of weeks and Louisa realized how truly alone she would be in these struggles.

She opened Shorter's desk and took out one of the long English cigarettes she knew he kept there. She knew this was the last little moment she had to enjoy herself and not worry about the rest of the day.

The wind slammed the door to Shorter's private bathroom closed with a loud snap. It startled Louisa out of her momentary bliss. She set the cigarette down in a copper ashtray that took up one of the corners of the large desk. She reached out carefully for the handle of the thick, wooden door and she felt an almost electric tingle run down the back of her neck."Hello? William?" She said timidly into the room.

William Shorter's body swung loosely from a thick brown belt attached to one of the golden fixtures drilled into the tile walls. The quiet breeze gave the body a slight sense of movement. His face was dark grey, his eyes still open and looking out at the world like glass beads. Louisa couldn't help but scream.

Louisa walked back to the desk, sat in the large leather chair and picked up her still lit cigarette. She took a deep breath and blew the smoke out upwards into the air. She hardly noticed as time passed and the cigarette burnt down to its end. William Shorter was a dear friend and she would miss him. But deep down in the back of her mind, Louisa knew what William's death meant. Louisa was running the studio now. This was her office.

She picked up the phone and dialed the girl working at the desk outside.

"Call 911. William Shorter is dead," Louisa said as calmly as she could.

She hung up before the girl could scream or ask any questions. That was it, that was how it had to be. Someone had to keep the ship running straight. She would die before she would let one of the financiers from New York ruin everything she had worked towards these last so many years.

Louisa McKay knew she was put on this earth to run this studio and in its own morbid way, William Shorter's death was the single best thing that could have ever happened to her. God bless the poor bastard, she thought to herself as she crushed the cigarette down into the ashtray. She hoped he knew what he was doing.

SEVEN

Cassie sat framed by the three bare bulbs hanging over the mirror in the small guest bathroom. Her back to the mirror, she struggled with the zipper on the dress Edith had leant her. She couldn't help feeling foolish as she struggled to squeeze into the evening gown. She hadn't been to an opera before and didn't think she would like it. The dress was too short and black with a white collar that dipped lower down her chest than she was used to.

A long slit came up the side of the dress, revealing Cassie's white thigh. She was painfully aware Edith was at least two sizes smaller than herself and had yet to decide if the dress should be considered comical or scandalous on her. She finally got the zipper all the way up and turned to face herself in the mirror, straightening the front of the dress with her hands.

She tilted her head in curiosity as she looked at herself. The dress almost fit. She snapped her mother's silver brooch around her neck and let her hair fall down from the tight bun over her pale shoulders. She had never worn anything so expensive and enjoyed the moment alone in the yellow light.

David let out a loud whistle as she walked

into the kitchen. Clyde gave a mostly respectable applause.

"Oh how wonderful!" Edith exclaimed as she rushed towards Cassie still standing in the door to the kitchen.

"I don't know, I feel a little silly," Cassie said pulling at the red bangs which framed her pretty face.

"You look beautiful," Edith said with a coy smile. Cassie walked the rest of the way over to David, who grabbed her by the waist and pulled her down into his lap. He kissed her for a long moment, smearing her oleander lipstick. "She's right you know, you look beautiful." David said.

"It's not too late for you two to stay here and spend a little time together," Clyde said with a grin. "But if you still want to go to the show we're supposed to meet the Blackerts in the lobby. We might want to get a move on."

The Blackerts were waiting downstairs in the lobby of the apartment building. They were arguing but quieted their voices when they noticed the two young couples enter the lobby. They turned to greet the couples and Phillip made a show of bowing to kiss Cassie and Edith's hand.

"You two certainly do look wonderful this evening," Phillip said in his old world accent.

Cassie couldn't help feeling self conscious in the small black dress in front of these strangers. But soon everyone was laughing and visiting and it seemed as if the evening was off to a fine start. Mrs. Blackert said something about how nice the dress looked but Cassie could hardly manage anything much more than a smile and nod with how strange and new everything seemed that evening. They had been to formal events in L.A. every once in a while. Movie premieres or a big dinner David would attend with men from overseas that had money and were looking for a place to spend it. Each time Cassie felt strange and out of place. Tonight was no different.

"Have any of you seen Baults performed before?" Phillip asked as he handed tickets to everyone.

"I'm afraid I've never even heard of Baults," Cassie said.

"It's a marvelous piece of composition. And I'll be damned if it isn't a wonderful show. I think you just might enjoy yourself," he replied with an old man's laugh.

"Phillip, leave that poor girl alone," Mrs. Blackert said in some sort of joke. The rest of the group laughed.

Clyde stepped outside and hailed a cab. It was a monster of a car and the six of them fit easily once the cabbie finally allowed David and Clyde to sit in the front of the large car. Phillip gave the man an address somewhere downtown and the car zipped towards the night. Cassie couldn't help imagining the opera house as an old baroque musicians paradise full of masquerade masks and glorious evening wear.

As they piled out of the cab, Cassie stared up at the building in wonder. The building had been glamorous once, but that was years ago. Paint was chipping off in places and the marquee had dozens of blown bulbs. The name of the opera hung in the bright black letters, some just barely legible. "Il Diavolo e la Fanciulla" the billboard read. Cassie wondered what the words meant.

Phillip paid the cabbie with a thick wad of bills. Cassie pulled the borrowed overcoat tighter around her small frame as she stood in front of the decaying old facade of the opera house. The front lobby of the room was darker than Cassie expected and full of people that all seemed roughly the Blackert's age. Cassie couldn't help but feel a bit exposed once she checked her coat and was glad when the lights dimmed in the atrium signaling that the show was about to start.

"Do you do stuff like this often?" Cassie asked Edith.

"Not really," Edith answered.

"That makes two." Cassie replied.

"I'm happy you two are staying with us. It's good to have a little company, I just wanted to make sure you knew that," Edith said quietly.

"Edith it's been wonderful staying with you. I just want you to know that we're always here for you."

Edith smiled back at Cassie and the two women were caught up in the line entering the theater. A pale old man in a frayed waistcoat tore their tickets and Cassie followed the Blackerts up a long strip of stairs to one of the oyster shell box seats that hung around the upper rim of the theater. They settled in just as the lights dimmed over the broad stage.

A single spot light came up, focused on the center of the stage. The orchestra hiding deep in the pit began tuning their instruments. A man in a long tailed tuxedo made his way to the spotlight and combed his long white hair off the shoulders of his jacket.

"Ladies and gentlemen, I want to thank you and welcome you this evening. We've got performers from every part of the globe and tonight will prove to be a beautiful and special evening. May I please have a brief round of applause for Baultz's The Devil and the Maiden, a study in madness, lust, envy and loss."

The man let a deep bow take his body and the spotlight disappeared. The orchestra finished tuning and the conductor took his place at the small podium. He tapped his small wooden wand a few times against the long side of his sheet music and a real and sudden silence fell over the large dim room.

The lights came up to just above darkness and a tall, beautiful woman walked onto the stage.

She began to sing in a deep, tenor voice. Slowly, different spotlights illuminated various parts of the set and it became clear the woman was standing at the gates of hell. The woman didn't know what had brought her to this portal but her voice was magnificent and Cassie somehow understood what the woman was singing even if she didn't know the language.

"She's from my hometown. Just south of the Austrian Border in Kitzbuheuel." Phillip Blackert leaned over and whispered into Cassie's ear.

The woman's voice filled the opera house, unaffected by its surrounding elements and still rising to the top of the cavernous space. The crowd was silent as her long solo wound through its loud and clamorous notes introducing the players and the situation. The song slowly came to an end and the lights dimmed around the stage. The woman disappeared, the orchestra players paused to turn the pages of their manuscripts, and the opera began again.

Cassie sat enchanted by the music and atmosphere. Every part of the evening a strange new world that she had never experienced. Cassie couldn't help but feel as if the woman was singing directly to her in the seat high above the stage. The lights got darker, the evening later, and the music louder.

Satan was played by an older singer. He was trying to lure the beautiful young woman into joining him in hell for the rest of eternity but the girl was constantly thinking of new ways to fend off his advances and turn his pursuits and powers to her own good.

Each act brought some new cunning pursuit of the devil towards the fair maiden and in each act she proved herself less and less innocent. First, she fooled the devil into running water back through the well that supplied the town. Thinking this was all that he had to do to convince the girl to accompany him to the afterlife, the devil gladly obliged and brought water back to the poor village after years of drought. The girl was hailed as savior of the village and the devil, having taken on a human form in his pursuits of the beautiful maiden, moped around the town disappointed in his failure.

Staccato sounds came up from the dark orchestra pit and filled the large opera hall. The dark air echoed with the devil's lust and the young woman's childish pranks. The crowd was silent in the darkness and the opera played out before them like some window into another time. Chorus after chorus performed by the members of the town's people and the girl's family warned her to quit toying with such a helpless man but the girl listened to no warning and kept the devil twisted around her fingers.

Cassie looked around in the dim room, she turned to David and held his hand in the balcony where they sat. His silhouette was cut out from the bright spotlights that lit the stage. He was enthralled and she could see him leaning in with excitement and eagerness at each little plot twist or change of musical key.

But more so, Cassie could feel the music effecting her, sweeping through her like a magnetic field. Bending her emotions and twisting them in the wind of the stringed instruments and the booming echoes of the singers on stage. She couldn't look away from the actor playing the devil on the stage. He was an older, tall man with a thin figure that seemed cut from plate steel. His voice had a timbre she hadn't heard before and she wondered if he had been some famous singer in Europe in his younger days. He played the part well and she felt for the devil in the story, willing to use his power to get his way but constantly being outsmarted by the strange girl.

The devil revealed himself to the audience in the form of an internal monologue that the townspeople could not, or would not, comprehend. Each time he was thwarted by the maiden, he got angrier and weighed his choices, reveal himself as the lord of the dead to the townspeople and take the woman by force or try his hand at the kindness which he felt so helpless against. Each time he tried some other act of charity for the small village his intentions were abused and he was made a fool. At his lowest, as the cruel and hurtful villagers drove the young man from the village and cursed him for his love towards a woman that would never love him back, the devil left down the lonely and dark road leading out of town. He promised to return one day as a different man and take his vengeance on the town and its people.

The maiden met him at the far end of the village and in a high and flowing solo piece she cast him out from her heart and town forever, wished he was dead, and called him a fool for ever having loved her. The devil turned and walked away alone, softly humming to himself.

The lights came up and the curtains rose for intermission. The crowd snapped out of the haze that had fallen over them during the first half of the opera. For the first time since the show started, Cassie let go of David's hand.

"Well, What do you all think?" Phillip Blackert asked.

"It's haunting," Cassie said softly.

"Interesting choice of words my dear." Blackert said.

"I don't know about you but I could use a drink. We've got a few moments before the show picks up again. Shall we?" Clyde asked as he held the curtain back to let the girls pass out into the red velvet hallway.

The opera house piped soothing music into the hallways between performances but Cassie found the thoughtless music annoying after the beauty and majesty of what they had just heard. The rest of the audience milled about in their fine black formal wear and wandered outside towards the cold night to smoke. Cassie didn't feel like standing in the cold and waited in the atrium, looking at the peeling paint falling off the old walls and the glowing crystal chandeliers that hung from delicate golden chains nearly a hundred feet above.

She watched through the windows as Mr. Blackert excused himself from the smoking crowd and came back in though the large glass revolving doors. His long black coat nearly touched the floor and he seemed as if he was specifically built for this time and place and to be anywhere else would be a waste.

"Are you enjoying yourself?" he asked with a slight bow.

"Quite. I've never done anything like this. I really want to thank you and Mrs. Blackert for the opportunity. David and I don't get dressed up too often, unless it's for some studio event," Cassie said with a blush.

"Well you seem quite at ease and you look beautiful to boot," He said.

"Thank you very much."

"We've got a few more moments before the curtain goes up again. Would you like to meet one of the singers? He's an old friend of mine."

Cassie decided to go along with the old

man out of fear of seeming rude. Phillip Blackert extended his arm and Cassie slipped her hand neatly into his. The fading opulence of the building fell away as Cassie crossed the threshold into the back of the stage. It was darker there and a surprising number of men and women worked in the dim shadows with large heaps of rope or costumes or props, silently preparing the show for its second half. Most of the people seemed to either know Phillip Blackert or at least not mind his being backstage and Cassie wondered if anyone could just walk in off the street.

They wound their way down the end of the building and past the large mess of rope that held the lighting fixtures towards the back of the stage. Stage hands and bit players smoked and drank cheap red wine in the few moments between performances. A few of the men looked at Cassie as she walked by and she felt self conscious of the expensive and revealing dress she wore. Phillip led them deftly down a hallway lit by one bare bulb and into the basement of the theater. They walked past the orchestra pit as men and women polished instruments and organized sheet music and argued between them selves about this or that.

They stopped in front of a small white door hanging loose on its hinges and Phillip rapped on it with his large knuckles. The door opened under the pressure of Phillip's hand and swung inward. The tall thin man sat outlined against the rows of bulbs that surrounded the mirror. He was playing a game of cards against himself and was pleasantly surprised to see them standing in his doorway.

He quickly stacked the cards and stood to greet Phillip and Cassie with great bravado.

"Thomas, we've just come down to congratulate you on a wonderful first act and to wish you well. This is my dear friend Cassie McClain, she's quite the fan of yours." Phillip said with a smile as he embraced his old friend.

Thomas bent low and took Cassie's hand in his and kissed it. Cassie blushed.

"It is quite the honor to meet you Ms. McClain," Thomas said at the bottom of his bow.

"I must admit this is my first opera," Cassie said as she pulled back her hand.

"It's not exactly Vienna but I do hope you're enjoying yourself," Thomas said.

"Well I've never been to Vienna so it seems very beautiful to me. Thank you so much for having us this evening."

"Thomas here was the one that provided our tickets. He tries to get us to come out any time he's playing New York. I'm just so glad you and David could join us this evening," Phillip said.

Thomas turned to take a seat at his dressing mirror, opening up a small drawer at the side of the table and taking out a pad of white make up.

"Please stay but excuse me while I get made up. We only have a few moments before the curtains go back up and I must prepare my face."

Cassie watched as he carefully dabbed under his eyes and over the flesh on his neck and hands. He took a black pad out and dipped the small applicator under his eyes and around the corners of his mouth giving a harsh pallor to his otherwise youthful face.

"Cassie here is in show business herself," Phillip said as he took a seat in the corner of the room.

"I work in the moving pictures, nothing so grand as what you do." she said.

"I'm sure the lights are still hot my dear," Thomas said as he put the finishing touches around his face and eyes.

"How do I look?" he asked.

"Like the very devil himself," Phillip answered.

"Well it certainly was a pleasure meeting you Cassie and I do hope you enjoy the end of the show," Thomas said. "Please excuse me."

Thomas took the long black cape off the hook next to the door and threw it around his shoulders. He paused to say something to Phillip in a strange language Cassie didn't understand and passed through the door. The room suddenly felt very cold to Cassie. She pulled the small jacket tighter around her frame and for just the briefest of moments she thought she saw her breath fog in the air.

"Shall we?" Phillip Blackert asked as he held

the door to the small dressing room open and pointed with his other hand back out into the thin crowded hallway.

They emerged from the same shabby door they had entered. David and Clyde were standing in the red carpeted lobby waiting for Cassie and Phillip. David had a glass of red wine for Cassie and one for himself.

"There you are. We thought the phantom of the opera might have gotten you," David joked as he handed Cassie the large glass of cheap red wine.

The lights in the lobby dimmed and came back up a few times, signaling the show was about to start. David quickly threw back the rest of his drink and Clyde did the same. Cassie took hers with them as they made their way back up the long, gilded stair case to the opera boxes. The lights dimmed in the stage room and the red black curtains split down the middle and fell back into the side of the stage.

"Something tells me it won't end well for the fair maiden," David whispered into Cassie's ear.

The orchestra finished tuning and the devil made his way out into the middle of the stage. It seemed like he was staring straight at Cassie but she was sure it was only her imagination. He started a brief, beautiful melody recounting the first half of the opera and layed out his plans for the village. He was to return just once more, in the form of an even sadder and more meek peasant to beg the village and fair maiden for a bit of kindness. A piece of bread, perhaps even love. If he is met with the same malice, he promised to bring the village down in flames around him. The music came to a crescendo and the devil disappeared as the stage hands reset the village background.

A few moments later, the devil was back on stage wandering into the village dressed as a sickly beggar. The sets of the small village came down on ropes around him as he walked the road leading to the village. Men and women sung about the toils in the field and their daily lives. The fair maiden sung about looking for love among the rich boys in the city to the north.

And just like before, when he approached anyone from the village he was met with disdain and contempt. As the musicians brought their instruments to a slow and weeping crescendo, the devil saw the girl picking flowers by a stream. He begged her for a piece of bread or a place to stay that evening and the girl simply pushed him into the river.

The spotlights turned red around the scene as the devil picked himself up out of the river. In a flash of light and a loud crash of cymbals, the devil struck the girl dead and took his real form. He was tall and regal and powerful and full of hate and revenge and the agony of fire.

The music changed, picking up in tempo and turning more hectic and frenzied. Cassie shifted in her chair as the lights shifted color and flashed.

The Devil made his way back to the village and began his revenge. Bright strikes of white hot light filled the auditorium as the devil brought down hellfire upon the little town. One by one, he struck down each of the villagers that had laughed at him or hurt him or found some excuse for not helping him. The music began to make Cassie dizzy and time after time she felt that Thomas, as the devil, was singing straight up to her, looking deep into her eyes and heaving all that emotion, all that anger at only her in the rafters.

The Devil made his way to the small farm on the outskirts of the town where the girl's parents lived. The musicians fell upon their instruments as if they themselves were possessed. The village burned in the distance. The father stood in the doorstep and told the devil he was sorry. The man asked for forgiveness for his daughter and his town.

A single violin picked up a low sad melody. After a few long moments, the devil echoed in his rapturous deep voice. He told the man that his daughter was dead and everyone he had ever known was dead. The devil let out a great laugh and the rest of the orchestra joined in, playing random notes at hectic intervals and building in volume.

With a snap of his finger the devil ignited a large flame in the palm of his hand and set it down on the doorstep of the small farm house. The man and woman inside as the house slowly caught fire around them. The red streamers and flowing paper that evoked the sense of fire slowly unfolded around the elaborate set never giving off the sense of something false, merely the sense of something true in some abstract form.

The musicians finally found their last few stanzas. The opera ended as the red black curtains came closing back in on themselves as the devil walked away from the burning village laughing to himself.

No one spoke for a moment as the audience sat in the sharp darkness. Cassie couldn't tell how long that moment stretched out but she was glad when the lights came back on and the curtains arose. Cassie might have been the first one to clap.

After a long period of applause, the devil and the maiden came out and took long bows in front of the crowd. The audience stood and gave the loudest applause to the pair. The curtains closed in front of them, pulling the stage back into that strange world unseen by audience eyes as the crews began to prepare again for the next day's performance. David turned to thank Phillip for the amazing seats at such an amazing performance and Phillip again shrugged off the thanks, saying that he was only glad to not have to attend the show all by himself. A soft spoken usher held a dim flashlight and signaled towards the exit.

Edith and David argued over their favorite parts and Clyde attempted an impression of the devil in the stairwell leading down to the lobby. Cassie was mostly silent, impressed and taken aback by the performance and just a bit confused by the man she had met in the dark recesses underneath the stage. She'd met all sorts of actors before and didn't think that the type could shake her but the man had genuinely seemed unlike anyone Cassie had ever met. Even with his age, she found him attractive.

Mrs. Blackert followed Cassie down the long spiraling staircase to the atrium and seemed to sense the impression of awe filling the young girl's mind.

"They put on quite a show, don't they?" She asked in her soft, slightly raspy voice.

"They certainly do. I just wanted to thank you and your husband again for inviting us to this show tonight, you hardly know us. I'm sure this sort of night wasn't cheap," Cassie said.

"You're young and you're beautiful, you shouldn't thank people that give you things," the old woman said with a laugh.

They reached the bottom of the stair case and Mrs. Blackert took Cassie's hands in hers as the rest of the group emptied out into the large, velvet carpeted opening of the theater's lobby.

"I want you and David to consider us friends. We'd do anything we could to help the two of you.

You should ask Clyde, we've got a few friends in the entertainment business and we've tried as hard as we can to help him. I'd like to think at least some of his success might be attributed to some calls we've made. We'd do anything we could for you and your husband."

"Oh, we're not married." Cassie said, pulling her hands back from the soft hold of the older woman.

"Oh that's fine, I'm sorry I didn't mean anything by it." She said with a laugh.

"Well thank you so much Mrs. Blackert. I truly appreciate it," Cassie said.

"Oh please dear, call me Nan, that's what all my friends call me." Mrs. Blackert said.

They cycled through the coat check and picked up their hand bags and coats. Clyde went outside and called them another one of the large yellow cabs and gave the rough Italian man the address to the apartment building.

They rode the elevator back up to the top floor. The bell chirped and the old man in the small red cap opened the door of the old machine. They emptied out into the long hallway. "Thank you again for the tickets," David said with an extended hand to Phillip. "I don't often get to show Cassie such a fine time."

"It was our pleasure," Phillip said.

Phillip turned and started down the long hallway, then paused.

"For that picture of yours, what sort of a place did you say you were looking for?" Phillip asked, his dark eyes beaming back at David and Cassie.

EIGHT

David piloted the red car across the large bridge that stretched out over fog and water. David was glad to be rid of Clyde. Once they were inseparable. Now David found the small character traits that made up the man childish and attention seeking. He knew his envy fueled some portion of the ill feelings towards his old friend. The large house, the new bride, the rush of attention found in a world driven mad by lights. Their friendship had been something else back in Korea. It was something simpler and easier to understand, the wait of sunset after sunrise, day after day. An endless marking of the calendar with a forced friendship found in a desperate situation of a war neither understood.

Cassie traced her finger along the blue interstate route that stretched from New York City to Colorado. The line crawled south and east down the paper, stretching over the ridged lines of mountains and into the center of the country. She couldn't help wondering if the hotel sat waiting for them next to the insignificant name on the map like an old treasure that had lost its polish.

"Do you think Clyde's going to get the part?" Cassie asked as she turned her head to watch the cars driving next to them.

"Not if he was the last actor in the world," David answered.

Three days later the red car climbed the last couple hundred miles of mountains and trees towards Cerberus, Colorado. Cassie had been crossing off the miles and now the red ink of her pen seemed as if it were to reach its inevitable conclusion.

The road was narrow and curved through tall aspen trees and snow covered strips of exposed mountain. They had stopped the day before to change the oil and buy chains for the car's tires. David was thankful they had as he steered through the white snow that came down in a thick solid mass around them. For miles, David slowly carved his way carefully through the narrow canyon that was left behind by the snow plows and other cars that ventured out onto the roads. Each time David began to get worried that they had been too long lost in the white chasm the snow would open up and reveal a small town or intersection that quietly assured them.

They stopped that night at a small hotel in one of the little ski towns dotted through the woods, hoping to wait out the storm and find fairer conditions the next day but white snow fell all night. When Cassie woke and pulled back the curtains, she couldn't help but admire the beauty of the frosted white trees covering the cold mountains.

As he drove, David lost himself in thought. He knew they were on to something. It was as if the world was technicolor, vivid with life and color and some other thing. He couldn't help but peer past Cassie's red hair and watch as she crossed mile after mile after mile off the large folding map. The white walls of snow on each side of the car fell away as the valley opened in front of them. On the far side, against the trees and the mountains covered in white snow, stood the Donan Hotel.

"David! It's just like Blackert said it would be. This is the place. You know this is the place!" Cassie screamed with excitement.

"You've got to be kidding me," David said. He could hardly believe his eyes.

It was as if the words from the script had found their way into some small Colorado town and formed themselves into something real from the rocks and woods of the mountain. The hotel held itself up in the lower tendrils of a great mountain with its back to the sun. The building's shadow stretched out across the green and white valley floor. As they drove closer, Cassie could make out the aspen gables that framed the structure's hard edges against the mountain. The large chimney brought steam and soot up from the building and melted the snow fall along the roof.

"Should I pull over. Do you want a picture from here?" David asked.

Cassie reached around the back of the seat

to pull up the blue camera bag, surprised it hadn't been the first thing to pop into her mind. She took the camera from its velvet package and held the lens up to the light to check for imperfections as David pulled the car off into a clearing at the side of the road at the top of the hill. The rush of cold air into the cabin of the car woke Cassie up and sent shivers down the back of her neck as she climbed out and stretched for a moment on the side of the road.

"Can you believe that?" she said.

David bent over and stretched the backs of his legs, the muscles rippling up against themselves as he fought off the uncomfortable hours of driving. It really was something spectacular, he thought to himself.

Cassie steadied her elbow against the hood of the car and framed the building in the camera's lens. The dark green and soft grey of the structure mimicked the world around it and the hotel fell into an easy frame between the sharp peaks of the mountains on both sides. The shutter snapped closed and Cassie pinched the lens cap back onto place.

"Shall we?" She asked turning to David.

The car pulled up under the great balcony that stretched out from the front of the hotel. Snow fell around the edge of the structure as David parked the car. A tall bellhop dressed in warm winter wear came out to greet them.

"Welcome to the Donan," he said with a curt smile.

"Thank you. I can't tell you how happy we are to be here. This place is beautiful," David said.

"It certainly is something." He turned back to face the couple, "Can I help you with your bags?"

The man loaded David and Cassie's few bags onto a copper plated rolling cart and followed behind them as they entered the old grand structure. The doors swung open, drifts of snow rushing in with the cold bursts of air. Cassie couldn't help but let out a small gasp as she walked into the great hall of the hotel's lobby. The room felt as if it existed in some other time, massive beams cut from huge pieces of timber stretched across the expanse of the open hall connecting in an angled peak at the center of the room. Rough, hand made iron work supported joined the timber at odd angles. No two joints exactly alike, a rough hewn beauty seemed to make the place only that much more significant. Ornate geometric patterns copied themselves along the thick carpet that filled the room, large octagons that seemed to swallow themselves whole as they reiterated down long hallways stretching out from the lobby.

A stair case stretched upwards to the high, second floor of the hotel. The banisters polished to a shining deep amber from years of travelers' gentle hands. A chandelier of massive elk horns entangled into a great mess of bulbs and bone hung from a thick iron chain above the center of the room casting just enough yellow light to give the room a warm and welcoming condition.

The porter took the bags through a small door into the inner recesses of the hotel, leaving Cassie and David alone in the hotel's lobby. David reached out and tapped the small copper bell. The pleasant tone echoed through the room. David looked over and smiled and shook his head at Cassie, grinning and wondering what they had gotten themselves into.

A door opened in the far corner behind the large oak desk and a man stepped out, buttoning the top button of his coat. He was short with neatly clipped grey hair and a matching mustache that stretched down the side of his mouth, framing his face in an appearance of both wisdom and curiosity.

"My my my, please excuse my absence. That's probably the first time in my entire career that I haven't been at the desk to greet a weary pair of travelers coming in from the cold. I am so very sorry."

"It's really not a problem. We're just happy to finally make it here." Cassie said.

"Welcome. How may I help you?" the man asked.

"We'd like to stay a couple nights. Actually we're here as location scouts for Worldwide Pictures," David said.

"How exciting."

"An acquaintance mentioned your hotel and we've driven half way across the country the last couple of days trying to make it here. I've got to admit, it's everything we could have ever hoped for," David said.

"We do aim to please," the man said with noticeable pride in his aging voice.

"If it's alright with you, we'd like to stay a few days, take some photographs and maybe talk to the owner about shooting here. Does that sound like something that might be a possibility? We're really not trying to put any pressure on you or your staff and I know some people don't think too highly of Hollywood so we wouldn't get our feelings hurt if you told us to scram," David said in coolly rehearsed voice.

"I don't see why that should be any problem. Of course I can't make any promises but I'm certain they would be excited at the prospect of the moving pictures coming to the Donan," the man answered

"Of course, we understand completely. We really just want to look around and get a feel for the place," Cassie said.

In the endless hours of driving across the states looking for this hotel, they'd had countless conversations about what they would say when they found a hotel that would work for their purposes. It was exciting for both of them to know that they had finally found something worth making a pitch for and it was equally exciting to know that both of them were following through perfectly on their vaguely rehearsed parts. Cassie threw a soft glance over at David as he stood in front of the desk clerk as the man turned and pulled a copper key with an engraved number 7 off the wall and handed it to David.

"It's one of the best rooms we have," the man said "A lot of the rooms are only open during the summer months. We don't get many visitors during the winter. As you probably know it's a bit treacherous getting over the mountain."

David slipped the key into the side pocket of his brown jacket. "I noticed. I thought we weren't going to make it ourselves there for a second."The halls stretched out in front of them in dizzying patterns and lengths. Everything either old rich carpet or hard wood stained dark with years of careful attention. The fixtures were a thick gold that stood out against the rich mahogany.

They made their way through the further wing of the hotel and found their room. Cassie turned the key to door number seven and dropped her bag at the threshold and the door opened, revealing a large well furnished room with a queen bed.

Cassie ran her hands along the foot of the bed. David ran his hand along her. He leaned close and kissed the back of her neck.

"Are you happy?" he asked.

She turned and kissed him.

A few hours later the sun was going down. Cassie stood in the window, wrapped in one of the soft white sheets from the bed. Light bounced off the far mountains and came in through the windows to fill the room.

David sat there and watched her, happy in the moment. Happy they'd finally found the place for which they'd been searching.

They walked outside towards the large clearing to get another view of the hotel while the sun was still up. The trees met boulders a few dozen yards from the rear door and the hotel's land fell quickly into the rocky chaos of the mountain. David and Cassie hiked up into the hills to look down at the hotel. It was much larger than it seemed from the road. The outline of the building stretched into an inverted M with the legs facing the bottom of the peaks to the south.

"Do you think this means they're gonna shoot the movie?" Cassie asked as she kicked a small rock down the ledge.

"I don't know but it certainly helps our chances. You did good, finding this place. It wouldn't have happened without you," David said.

"Thanks, I just can't believe that it was here all along," She blushed a little and walked away.

Back in from the cold, Cassie stepped in to the marble bath tub and instantly pulled her foot back from the steaming water. She turned the handle back towards the cold water. David was in the other room hanging his laundry and getting dressed for supper. She pulled her hair up around her neck, folding it in her hands like a golden knot and stepped into the water. A rush of calming hot water fell over her body and for the first time in months she felt relaxed and calm, her mind empty and without worry. Those long weeks of calling to report another failed attempt. Things with David getting more and more rushed. A relationship slowly turning into a business partnership. But everything seemed better now. They hadn't even told the home office yet, but something seemed to settle all of that inside Cassie's mind. Slowly her thoughts and worries slipped from her mind and she sank further down into the hot water.

Cassie saw a vision of dozens of people dressed in tuxedoes and flowing gowns rushing out of the Donan's large dining hall. Dark smoke flowed from the dining room out the door's and spread along the ceiling like oil. In the midst of the chaos a young boy had been pushed to the floor. He was crying and struggling to stand, but each time he rose the crowd of screaming people pushed him back down. Cassie watched, painfully aware she could not help but also not look away, as the boy's head was crushed under the leather dress shoe of a man struggling to pull off his burning tuxedo jacket.

David knocked on the bathroom door and Cassie's mind snapped back into itself and she twisted the water off, shaking just slightly as the cold mountain air hit her skin.

The table was already made up for them in the large dining room. More than a dozen chandeliers had been refitted to accept electric bulbs but the room still seemed lit by yellow candles.

A few guests sat sparsely spaced in the large dining room. David looked around to see what kind of clientele the hotel attracted but he couldn't seem to find a pattern to the room. An old couple sat in the corner giving the impression of a lifetime of good memories and fond friendships between the two of them. The woman told a story wildly with her hands while the man laughed quietly into his pea soup. On the other end of the hall, another couple almost the same age as David and Cassie sat drinking red wine. A young waiter with jet black hair folded silverware into large white napkins as the the restaurant went on about its business.

A tall woman in a long brown dress brought them menus and glasses then disappeared into the further reaches of the restaurant. David couldn't help but watch her go. Cassie ordered a bottle of wine, the cheapest on the menu, and they fell into the familiar routine of mixing work and pleasure.

First, they would have to get the photographs developed. She wanted to make sure they got the proofs back to the main office in Los Angeles before the long weekend coming up in a few days. David assured her that there were going to be plenty of time to get the photos in the mail and asked her to please calm down. The waiter in the dark jacket brought the wine over to the table and poured a small glass for Cassie to taste.

David and Cassie ordered food and sat in the large dining hall and watched a thunder storm roll in over the mountains. It started with bright flashes on the far side of the peaks. Then the lights filled the entire valley out in the flat stretch of earth immediately in front of the Donan. Each time the lightning struck, it lit the entire dining room through the large plate windows.

David pretended he could predict the timing of the hot strikes of light with some elaborate pattern and tried to perfectly clap his hands in time with the lighting strike. The wine had come and gone and both Cassie and David were enjoying themselves. They ordered another bottle. Inwardly, both were celebrating having found the hotel without beginning to hate one another. And then, after half a dozen or so failed attempts, David finally clapped his hands at the exact same moment as the large room filled with the white light from the storm's flash.

"Magic," David said holding his hands out in front of himself.

Cassie stumbled out from the large door

into the moonlight bouncing off the peaks of the mountains. The door closed for a second as David stood and pulled his jacket on, Cassie stood alone in the moonlight on the wooden walkway stretching out into the shadows at the base of the mountain, her white dress stood out in reverse silhouette against the dark greens and blacks of the mountain. For a moment, David stood admiring her. The white fog of the mountain rolled down the hills and came over the thick pine beams that made up the guided walkways stretching out from the hotel. Lightning struck off to the northwest and Cassie's form was taken over by the fog for a moment that stretched out for an eternity.

The rain started a moment later and Cassie turned to run back towards the door, holding her hands above her head. She cried out with a combination of joy and annoyance. By the time she made it to the door she was soaked through, her dress hanging tightly to her body.

The cold mountain water fell from her hair and dress onto the floor in small puddles as they a crossed the lobby heading back towards their room.

"Have a lovely evening," The concierge said to them as the crossed the hall.

David shut the door behind them as Cassie pulled the soaking dress up over her head and threw it onto the floor. Her hair was dripping wet and her black underwear hung close to her body.

She looked up at David with large brown eyes full of affection and attraction and friendship. They went to bed and didn't rise until late the following day.

In the small dark moments before each drifted off to sleep they halfway promised to make sure the photographs got developed. Tomorrow, tomorrow would be soon enough.

NINE

The phone calls hadn't stopped for the last three days. The promotion had been made effective by the board but Louisa was still getting used to the responsibilities that came along with the new job. She'd hardly slept more than 4 hours since Shorter's death.

The funeral service had been pleasant. The kind words were said that everyone expected. The sun shone constantly that day. The coast seemed like an ironic place for a funeral. Shorter's wife was there along with his two children.

The heads of the other studios came to pay their respect. Louisa didn't speak to anyone and had one hard drink at the wake before heading home.

The next day, Louisa's secretary gave Louisa a large pile of folders on her way into the office. She sat down at her desk and idly flipped through the documents as she ran down a long mental checklist making sure that there wasn't anything else to do.

One of the folders caught her attention. Inside was a number of black and white photographs and a note from David. It read simply. "We've found it. Donan Hotel, Cerberus Colorado. You're welcome."

Louisa picked up the phone and dialed with one hand, still flipping through the photographs as she waited for the call to connect.

"It's Louisa, get Bradshaw in this afternoon. We've got something."

The secretary answered in a muffled response. Louisa asked for a fresh pot of coffee to be brought in and hung up the phone. There was a lot to be done.

Bradshaw sat in his home, facing the window that looked out into the canyons, a glass in one hand and a 5x7 photograph in the other. The house was still and seemed as if not even the air in the large open room moved. He sat, lost in thought when the phone began to ring. He didn't move, didn't even acknowledge the sound filling the room. The answering machine finally clicked over and answered the call.

"Bradshaw, sorry. Mr. Bradshaw, this is the office of Louisa McKay from Worldwide. We think that we have found the location for your film. We just wanted to coordinate getting you the reports and documents. If you could send someone to pick up the documents this afternoon it would be splendid. You can call me back at this number or I'll try back in a few hours. Thank you." The tin voice of Louisa's assistant insisted.

The phone clicked off and Bradshaw took another sip from the dark glass. He looked down at the photograph of Cassie standing in the door frame of the Donan hotel, soaked in her wet dress. David stood a little inside the door watching her, his back to the camera. Bradshaw fingered the torn corner of the photograph, picked up the phone and started to dial Louisa McKay's personal number.

Louisa pulled the green car around the road's sharp corners as she drove out to meet James Castle for lunch at Murphy's, one of the fancy places hustlers took lunch. Like a lot of people, Louisa despised Castle. Simply put, he was one of the bad ones, part of what gave the town something of which to be ashamed.

Louisa had looked over the budget of the Bradshaw film once the police and the accounting department were done with it. She knew just enough to know that both she and the studio were both in a pretty precarious position after the way Shorter had left things.

The accountants had found Shorter's artistic bookkeeping a few days after he died. In some ways, it eased people's minds to know he had taken his own life to deal with his own problems. People preferred insulation.

The movie was put on temporary hold while the finances were settled. Nothing out of the ordinary, these things happened with a strange frequency in the glamorous town. But Louisa knew they were in a much more precarious position than even the heads of the Worldwide knew. So much of the studio's assets were tied up on the long shot of Bradshaw's new prestige picture that the studio had crossed the point of no return. Costs had become too great to abandon ship. To quit now would cost the next two and half years of production budget and the studio would be forced back into B westerns and skin flicks until they worked their way back in with the big five studios. Louisa had no intention of losing ground. There was only one path forward from here and that was to get this picture finished. For that, she would need Castle's help.

James Castle was already at the table when Louisa got to the restaurant. He was dressed in a dark blue suit of thin cotton and sat drinking a steaming cup of tea. He stood and kissed Louisa on the cheek when she said hello.

"James, a pleasure," She said with a small curtsey.

"It's good to see you Louisa, you look as lovely as ever" Castle said with that same half smirk Louisa remembered hating so much.

They took their seats and a waiter brought Louisa a cup of coffee.

"Congratulations, and my condolences of course. It was terrible to hear about Shorter. But I'm happy to see you seem well," Castle said looking over his glasses that hung low on the bridge of his nose.

"I'd be lying if I said I hadn't thought about

getting his job someday," Louisa responded.

Castle raised his tea glass in the air and Louisa met his eyes. Their cups softly clinking in celebration.

"To what lies ahead," Castle said.

"To what lies ahead," Louisa replied.

The lunch was fine, overpriced but to be expected. Louisa knew that he would push the bill on her but she had already accepted it mentally. The conversation had idly drifted between rumors floating through the movie town. Louisa attempted to get him comfortable with her once again. They had worked together many years back when Castle was in publicity and Louisa worked under one of the old heads of Worldwide as an young assistant. She remembered Castle had been good at his job, quick witted and seemingly able to get any bad press under control before the eventual and inevitable consequences of Friday night found its way into Monday's morning paper. She hadn't liked him then either. She was always unsure of what hid under the slicked back hair and quick one liners that came so neatly at cocktail parties up in the hills.

"We've got a picture, it's the new Bradshaw film. We're looking for a partnership," Louisa said when she found an appropriate opening in the conversation.

Castle's sat up a little straighter in his chair, Louisa could see a glint in his eyes as he quickly added up possibilities in his head.

"Why do you need us? Why not just do it yourself?" Castle asked.

This was the moment in which she had to appeal to his ego, get him and his company's money on board without making it appears as if Louisa was out of options.

"It would be a good match," she said coolly.

She let the words sink in for a moment and wondered if she had been wrong about this man and the financial situation of Eagle, the small studio that Castle now worked for. They'd been on the up and up for the last couple years and Louisa knew that they were hungry to move into territory reserved for larger studios. She was offering them exactly what she hoped they wanted.

"We know you want to get into bigger pictures. A chance at real money, but you're stretched thin and your roster doesn't stack up."

Castle was silent for a moment. His hand brushed at something on his blue pant leg.

"We need each other," Louisa said in the most even and confident tone she could hit.

"I'm glad you called Louisa," Castle answered.

TEN

The phone started to ring just as David popped back into consciousness from a deep sleep. He reached over Cassie and picked up the phone. It was the hotel attendant at the desk downstairs.

"Mr. Bannon. I'm so sorry, I hope I didn't wake you."

"No no. It was time to get up anyways."

"I was just calling to let you know that the groundskeeper is in today and he would be more than happy to show you around the hotel this afternoon. When I mentioned the prospect of Hollywood coming to our sleepy hotel his eyes lit up. He asked what he could do to help, I thought that this might be a good way."

"Thank you for thinking of us. What time should we meet him?" David asked as he reached for his wristwatch hanging loosely from the mahogany bed post.

"He's finishing up his morning routine around the grounds and should be ready for you both just after breakfast. Would that be acceptable?"

"That'd be perfect, thanks you so much. We'll be down in a few moments."

David hung up the phone and fell back into his pillow. The sound woke Cassie and she rolled over on the white pillow to look up at David with her big brown eyes still heavy with sleep.

"Who was it?" She asked.

Cassie packed two of her wider lenses and an extra roll of film into her small camera bag before they walked out of the door of the hotel room. David carried a leather case to take notes.

They ate a small breakfast of fruit and bread and made their way to the front desk. Sitting on one of the small benches running along side the great hardwood walls that stretched into the hotel, an old man with a bald head pulled on the base of his long white beard. He whistled a soft melody to himself, seemingly unaware of whoever else happened to be in the lobby. His head moved back and forth matching time with the soft melody.

The man stood up and stopped whistling. He took a step towards David, his hand extended and a smile on his face. His large, friendly smile revealed more than a few missing teeth, though it hardly diminished the man's pleasant demeanor. Cassie shook the man's hand and noted the many callouses and strong muscles stood out in contrast to his otherwise elderly appearance.

"Hi, I'm Eddie Cannahan. Groundskeeper here at the Donan. Goin' on just about 28 years at it if I've been going for a day."

"I'm Cassie and this is David. We're pleased to meet you, I can't thank you enough for taking time out of your day to show us around a little."

"It's my pleasure."

His voice had a faint but hard to place accent and although already covered in dirt and snow by mid morning, Cannahan carried himself with an air of elegance.

They started towards the large glass doors that swung out into the crisp morning air. The last bits of white glass morning fog were burning off around the green and slate gray peaks that surrounded the hotel and all three paused for a moment as the white frost filled their lungs.

A bit away from the hotel, Eddie paused and the three turned to take in the majestic sight. The eaves of the hotel bright white against the dark mountain behind it. The large peak of the central tower standing high above the tree line gave the hotel an appearance both elegant and severe.

"She's quite a sight isn't she?" Eddie said, breaking the silence.

"You have no idea how long we were searching for a place like this," Cassie said, almost unable to pull her eyes away from the beautiful scene.

Eddie turned and walked further out towards the grounds.

"All this time, it was right here waiting for ya," he said, mostly to himself.

"I guess it was," Cassie said as she and David turned to follow Eddie into the large expanse of the Donan's grounds.

At the far side of a clearing to the west, immediately in front of the hotel, Eddie's green

Ford '41 sat parked under a large cluster of pines, its hardwood flatbed covered in tools and strapped down with sets of thick ropes. The door caught just slightly as he tried to open it for Cassie but a quick pop to one of the joints with his thick fist settled the hinges and he extended a hand to help her climb into the large truck.

"Sorry, I don't give tours very often."Eddie turned the key over in its socket and the old car took off down one of the white gravel maintenance roads that criss crossed the grounds towards the mountains. Cassie sat between the two men, the three of them packed tight into the cab. The windows were down and the clear mountain air came in as they made their way to some of the smaller buildings at the foot of the mountains. Cassie looked up to notice a small, tattered black and white photograph of a man taped to the visor above the drivers seat, its edges frayed and torn.

"Is that your father?" she asked.

"It is. That was the first Edward Cannahan. He came here from Scotland in 1905 with the Admiral."

Eddie turned the old wooden knob on the radio and a soft big band tune started to play from the tin speaker.

"Who's the Admiral?" David asked.

"Admiral Pike. He built the hotel. He came over from Scotland in 1905, he'd made a fortune chasing pirates from the British seas in the 1800's and came over here looking to secure his place in the new world. Rich as he was, a Scot still couldn't hold much class in London."

"My father was in a wee bit of trouble back in Scotland and Pike offered him a stake in the hotel if he came in as his strong right hand. Those two men cleared the foot of this valley alone, working straight through the winter of '06 for enough lumber and land to start building the hotel when the snow melted that spring. Just two of them and a couple of broad-saws. It was a real feat."

"What kind of trouble was your father in?" Cassie asked.

"He never talked about it and passed away in '41, but when the Admiral was still around he'd make certain jokes about what a hound dog my father had been back in Scotland. So there's a good chance it had something to do with a woman."

"A lot of good stories do." David said, nudging Cassie lightly in the ribs.

The car came to a stop at another set of buildings on the far side of a large pine forest from the hotel.

"Cartwright said to show you everything, so I figured this would be as good a place to start as any. This is the maintenance grounds. That's my residence right over there," He pointed to a small but sturdy looking building facing the mountain with a small porch attached to the front of it.

"Not a bad view," Cassie said.

"The job has it's perks," Eddie smiled back. "This is where we do whatever maintenance we can, repairing the vehicles and a small amount of smith work. Welding, that sort of thing."

"You do all this on your own?" Cassie asked.

"I've got a little help. But mostly it's just me. The old hotel likes to take care of herself. We're lucky, the cliff face to her back braces most of the hard snow off her so we only have to deal with the soft stuff that comes from straight down. Nothing too bad has happened in a long time. We've been lucky since the fire."

As if on cue, two large hounds came bounding from behind one of the buildings, jumping and playing in snow. Eddie bent down to scratch the dogs behind the ears. Each dog was larger than any Cassie had ever seen. "54 people died. Mostly the maids and cooks, a rich family from New York visiting for the winter. The snow was falling so hard that the fire trucks couldn't make it up the mountain. The admiral and my father made it out and stood in that clearing, watching the whole hotel burn to the ground," Eddie threw a stick a little distance away and the two dogs leapt through the thick snow after it.

They walked a little closer to the buildings. A massive set of elk horns stretching most of ten feet across hung on the side of a red painted wall.

"The Admiral started rebuilding the hotel the next day. Parts of the building were still smoldering. He didn't care. He built it just the same, didn't change a thing. A lot of people thought he went mad watching the fire bring down the hotel. I think they were wrong. I think he might have always been insane, people never understood that."

"When did the hotel burn down?" David asked.

"It was in early '41. The depression was still going on. I was just a boy, but I remember most of it. It was so hot it melted the snow off the trees for almost a mile. You could feel it burning your face if you looked at it for too long. We packed our bags that night. I thought that we were going to leave, my father was still alive then. He and the Admiral had some sort of argument. I remember thinking they were going to kill each other. But we never left. The next day they just started building."

David looked over at the hotel, imagining the great building engulfed in flames. The paint and lacquer feeding bright yellow fire. The unflinching Admiral standing with his dark profile cut from the fire like a silhouette in absence of form itself, watching what he'd built disappear. David felt the temperature rise on his skin, as if the air was hot around him. A strong wind came from the east that shook the trees and cooled him off again. David rushed to catch up to Eddie and Cassie.

They walked out into the cold white and green forest, stopping once or twice to regain their breath and drink from a small canteen Eddie had brought with them. The path led up the east side of the mountain, winding its way back in on itself. They walked in silence, concentrating on the stones and loose gravel that made up the path.

"It's not too much further," Eddie said between calm measured breaths pulling at the thin mountain air.

The path leveled out and the trees opened to a plateau at the peak of a rocky outcrop. David bent over to catch his breath after the long hike. Cassie walked straight out to the large, flat rock amazed at the sight.

Beneath her, the valley opened up like an oil painting. The white outline of the Donan stood out sharply against the green and gray of the trees and mountains, placed expertly in the clearing so as to balance the scale and scope of the valley against itself. The hotel seemed like an extension of the mountain, something meant to be from the start. A structure more grown than built, as if glaciers sliding south had somehow carved the wood and iron from the mountain itself.

"It sure is a sight, isn't it?" Eddie said after a few moments.

"It certainly is," Cassie said, unable to take her eyes away.

"I figured this would be a good way to start the tour. The people around here are excited at the prospect of getting the moving pictures out here.

If you're serious about it we'll do everything we can to make it work. It'd be good for the hotel. It'd be good for all of us out here."

Eddie handed David the canteen. The young man took a small sip of the cold, clear water.

Eddie walked up to the edge of the bluff and threw a small stone out into the air. It fell with a soft echo. Cassie took the lens cap from her camera and framed the valley beneath her. The shutter clicked softly.

"Let me take a picture of you two," Eddie said.

Cassie handed him the camera and walked over to David in the center of the stone bluff overhang. David put his arm around Cassie's waist and kissed her softly on the top of her head. Eddie lifted the camera to his eyes and struggled to focus the lens.

"Sorry, it's been a while," He said, twisting the camera in his hands and looking for the correct button to press the shutter down. Eddie lifted the camera to his eye and clicked the shutter release.

"You two certainly make a pair. You're gonna have good looking kids you know that?" Eddie said.

Cassie blushed and smiled as she took the camera back.

"We're still kind of working up to that but thanks, we appreciate it," David said.

"Are you married Mr. Cannahan?" Cassie asked.

"Married? Of course I'm married. I'm married to that monster down there," Eddie said, pointing over his shoulder to the Donan behind him.

"I've been married to her my whole life practically."

They turned and started the long walk back down the mountain.

Eddie parked the green truck a little ways off from the large portico that covered the front of the hotel. Eddie held the large oak doors open for David and Cassie.

"The first version of the hotel went up in 1906, with construction completed the following summer and the first guests moving in for July 4th, 1907," Eddie said as they walked through the large foyer. Eddie waved to Cartwright at the front desk and they continued on the tour.

"The Admiral ran with Europe's movers and shakers so there's been a long list of famous and notable guests at the Donan over the years. We've had 3 princes, a sheik, 3 presidents, and people like to say Bonnie and Clyde stayed here under false names for a long weekend once, but that one's a little hard to prove. I'm of the mind that it's true but that may be one of the small sad facts lost to the churning tides history."

"If it makes a good story it might as well be true," David said with a smile.

"Well come on then, plenty more good stories where that came from," Eddie said as his pace quickened and they moved on through the hotel.

"This is the Grand Ballroom. One of the first rooms completed and rumored to be where the fire started back in '41. At least a few of the souls lost died right here. Through some damned bad luck or hell, maybe malice, someone had accidentally blocked the doors and 9 of the 14 lost in the fire died where we stand now."

Cassie and David entered the great hall a few steps behind Eddie. A large crystal chandelier hung from its golden chains. The hard wood floors had the worn sheen of years of care and use. The darker oak criss crossed with the lighter hard pine native to the area and formed a beautiful, almost dizzying pattern on the large floor that stretched all the way across the room. The walls were a soft golden and purple patterned wall paper with delicate wood trim lining the ceilings. "The room has been known to hold upwards of a thousand people on special occasions. Most notably, the New Years Eve celebrations for which the Donan has become somewhat infamous," Eddie said as they made their way through the large room.

Eddie reached a set of large stainless steel doors."And this is the kitchen. At the peak of the season we staff upwards of 25 cooks, bread makers, and assistants on site and have the full capabilities of serving hundreds of guests. Any number of weddings, banquets, and other celebrations have been served out of this great kitchen and I can honestly say most if not every single one of them left full, hopefully drunk, and more than satisfied with their meal," Eddie explained as they wound their way through the large kitchen.

"The large walk in freezer was redone a few years ago and we keep enough stock on hand to make it two or three weeks in case the roads ice over, which has been known to happen every once in a while."

Cassie snapped a few more photographs and David took notes in his yellow pad. Eddie hardly stopped moving long enough for them to gather all the information before shuffling them off to the next room. The doors opened out of the kitchen into the bar. It was a long dark wood bar with deep red details. Brass stools lined the bar that seemed to stretch fully out to the horizon and stood polished in a bright golden glow. "This is called the Blanton Bar. Supposedly after one of the Pirates the Admiral was rumored to have caught off the coast of Africa."

"It's a good name, rolls right off the tongue," David said.

"When we're really up and running 10 barmen work the bar and we can hold at least a couple of hundred. No one remembers the room having been full, but I'm sure it must have happened at some point."

David sat down at one the bright brass stools. "Well, what do you recommend?" Eddie opened the cantilevered top of the bar back and threw a red towel over his shoulder. Standing in front of the large collection of old looking bottles and pulling at his white beard, the old man seemed in his element.

"I'm glad you asked," Eddie said.

Eddie carefully pulled a pair of unmarked bottles down from their places on the large shelves and set them on the bar. He opened a drawer and took an orange from a chilled refrigerator and cut it in half. He poured equal measures of the two dark liquids into a large stainless steel glass and squeezed the larger half of the orange in after them.

"We call this the Fire of '41. For obvious reasons," he said as he turned to pull a large spoon from the drawer. He stirred the concoction then cracked an egg over the silver cup quickly. He let only the white drop into the cocktail then tossed the rest beneath the bar.

"You look like you've done this before," Cassie said as she snapped a picture of Eddie behind the bar.

"Just once," he said laughing. "Before I was in charge of the grounds I used to work the bar on busy nights. It was hard but I loved it. Seeing all the people coming in dressed to the nines. They were good, good days back then."

"And these aren't?" David asked.

"Oh they're good, they're always good, it's just

a little different than it used to be," Eddie said.

"How?" Cassie asked.

Eddie shook the drink hard with one hand high above his head. The ice rattled against the side of the shaker and when he was done Eddie rapped the shaker against the side of the bar, breaking the pint glass off the metal cup. He poured the frothy mixture into three short glasses with a few cubes of ice in each.

"Here," He said pushing the frothy auburn mixture toward the couple in the brass stools across the bar.

She coughed just slightly as the first sip hit the back of her throat. David and Eddie laughed softly at her.

"What the hell is in this?" Cassie asked as soon as she gotten her breath back.

Eddie turned and put the two unmarked bottles back onto the shelf and wiped his hands with the red towel draped over his shoulder.

"Sorry. Trade secret," Eddie answered with a coy smile.

David held his glass up in the middle of the dark bar. Cassie and Eddie followed, the glasses clicked together softly. The sound drowned out in the large room.

"To what comes next," David said with a smile.

"May it be as rewarding as we all might wish," Eddie added, throwing the rest of his drink back with one sharp motion.

Cassie tried to finish her drink but could hardly keep up.

"I'm sorry, it's delicious but just a bit strong for me," She said, struggling to hold back a hiccup.

"It's not a problem my dear," Eddie said as he cleared the glasses from the bar into one of the empty sinks built into the underside of the bar.

They laughed for a while longer. Eddie told them strange and funny stories of his childhood on the hotel grounds. David and Cassie found themselves holding their sides with laughter. David told a few of his rowdier stories from his younger days in Hollywood and Eddie laughed as hard as they were after long. The Fire of '41 was put safely back up on the shelf and a bottle of bourbon was poured liberally into the remaining glasses. "You two really are a breath of fresh air around here," Eddie said.

"Well thank you for saying that. We're just so excited that you guys seem receptive to the idea. You have no idea how long we've been on the road" Cassie said.

"It's fine, it's really my pleasure. When Charles wired me saying you guys were on your way to the Donan, I didn't really know what to expect. But I've got to admit you've really exceeded my wildest dreams," Eddie said pouring himself another large glass of the auburn bourbon.

David drank the rest of his glass. Cassie

pushed her tumbler a little back towards the center of the table and sat up a little straighter on the brass stool.

"Charles?" she asked.

"Charles Blackert, in New York, he wired a week or two ago saying you two were on your way out here and that you were excellent company, of which I must tell him he was spot on in his assessment," Eddie answered.

"You know Charles Blackert?" Cassie asked.

"Of course, he's my half brother," Eddie said, tipping the glass back and looking sharply into Cassie's large brown eyes.

ELEVEN

Louisa brushed the black wool of her suit pants tight against the side of her leg. She'd waited outside the office for close to an hour.

Louisa couldn't tell if they were testing her. God damn it Shorter, this was your job. You were supposed to take care of this so the rest of us could do the real work, Louisa thought to herself. She knew it was too late for that kind of thinking. She looked over the last of her projections stretching out to the end of the year and brushed at the wrinkles in her slacks again. With help from Castle they would make it into production on Bradshaw's film and limp into next year with heads high, even if a little worse for the wear.

She was proud of the deal she'd struck with Castle's company, Eagle Films. She'd spent years trying to outdo her competition leaving her with exact knowledge of what sort of leverage to apply and where it would hurt the most. She'd pulled off a real piece of magic. That deal should have been impossible and her division of Worldwide should have been left for dead. She had made fire where there was none. People would notice, they had to. She just had to bring in the Bradshaw picture on time and on budget.

She wiped at some sweat beading up on her

forehead. The suit was too heavy for Los Angeles. She should have known better. She took a deep breath and waited, hoping the board members would see what a miracle she had pulled off.

Through the frosted glass window of the board room, Louisa could see the figures standing up and shaking hands with one another. The meeting seemed to be over and a few moments later the door began to open.

William Bradshaw stood framed in the doorway, shaking hands and laughing lightly with the men that ran the parent company of Worldwide studios. His messy hair and untucked shirt disgusted Louisa. She stood up, folded the leather attache of notes and graphs under her elbow and took that first, nearly impossible, step towards a man that never ceased to ruin her days.

"Bradshaw," Louisa said with a nod to the recluse director as she stepped past him into the board room. Turning to the other men, she extended her hand."I'm Louisa McKay, head of Worldwide Pictures."

The taller of the three men took her hand in a solid grip and smiled back at her.

"We've heard a lot about you. Come on in," he said.

"Pleasure to see you Louisa," Bradshaw said to Louisa with a curt turn. He walked down the hallway and turned towards the elevators.

The tall man motioned for Louisa to sit at

the head of the table. The tall man was Frank Lean. Sitting next to him was the representative from the Japanese holding company that had purchased a controlling stake in Worldwide 6 ago, Takeda Hiromoto. The shorter balding man with red skin around his paunched face had to be the owner of the company himself, William Mabry. He'd started Worldwide in the early twenties back when silent films were still king and was rumored to have fist fought Harry Warner for rights to one of the early Chaplin films. Whatever composure Louisa had left after nearly an hour waiting in the sticky leather chair outside this boardroom quickly left her. She hoped no one noticed and spread the attache out on the desk in front of her.

"I just want to start with saying, we're damn proud to meet you. We've heard a lot about you," Frank Lean said, his voice high for such a large man.

"Thank you. It's a pleasure to be here," Louisa said honestly.

Lean went through the motions of introductions and Louisa nodded politely after each name and handshake. She shuffled her papers, unsure of where to start. The Bradshaw film was on top, but she couldn't help the strange sinking feeling in her stomach.

"With introductions behind us, let's get down to it. We know about your deal with Castle, I just want to say 'Whoa!'. You really pulled a fucking rabbit out of your hat," Lean said pouring himself a glass of water from the sleek pitcher in the center of the table.

The room seemed to cool off 30 degrees and Louisa thought she could feel the tension release all the way down her spine.

"It was a work of art. Really, it was. Unfortunately, we're not going with Eagle. Which actually works out very well for you," Lean said.

For the second time that day, the clock stood still and Louisa thought she might faint. She must have misheard him. His high, simpering voice must have somehow clouded his meaning. "I'm sorry sir, I'm not sure I understand," Louisa said in the most reverent voice she could muster.

"I couldn't have done any better myself. And I assure you, I very, very rarely say that," the small man at the far side of the table said as he looked out the window without facing Louisa or acknowledging her presence.

"You were right to do what you did. Shorter, God rest his dim witted soul, nearly ruined us. You stopped that, you saw what was going on and you did what you had to do. Even if it meant swallowing your pride and asking for help. That's right isn't it?"

Mabry said, still looking out the window.

"Initiative. I like that." "I'm sorry, I'm not sure I understand."

"Oh my dear, I'm so sorry. You don't even

know what we're talking about. A thousand apologies. We've been in here for most of the morning nailing down this deal. Of course you don't know," Mabry said, laughing softly to himself.

"Don't know what?" Louisa asked, trying to keep the anger out of her voice.

"Bradshaw secured his own financing," Takeda said, finally breaking his long silent streak.

"What? What are you talking about?" Louisa could feel herself losing the cool sharp edge she prided herself on.

"We're not even fully sure how he knew what going on inside Worldwide. But he seems to have understood what Shorter was doing for him and been aware of the financial shortcomings of the studio. He came to us with funding for the picture. Rest assured no one is going to forget what a hat trick you pulled with Castle, but needless to say, it's pointless now. No reason to give the competition a leg up," Lean said coolly.

"What are you talking about? Why didn't he come straight to me?" Louisa could feel the anger welling up inside her. Her frustration with Bradshaw reached a new climax of angst and bile and the softest brand of hate.

"Time was an issue and he thought it best to bring his investors straight to us. Bradshaw and I go way back," Lean said in a reassuring tone.

"So that's that? Our problems are just solved out of nowhere?" Louisa asked in disbelief.

"To put it simply, yes," Mabry answered.

"Who put up the money?" Louisa asked.

"It's a fund from Scotland. Not too well known, but they have means and are interested in branching some of their investments out. It's unclear how Bradshaw got involved with them, but their check has cleared and the money is in our accounts as of 45 minutes ago," Mabry said.

Louisa was speechless. She felt the blood fall from her face. The Castle deal had been the crown jewel of the last 10 years of her career and it had been eclipsed simply and completely. Her hard work was for nothing. She couldn't help but feel redundant.

"Thank you," Louisa said flatly.

"Sometimes that is all a person needs to know," Mabry said back to her from across the large table.

Frank Lean poured himself another glass of water but didn't drink any of it.

"We wanted to meet you and let you know that you deserve Shorter's office. You're the only person that can fill his shoes. This Bradshaw film has gotten away from us, all of us. We wanted to talk face to face to get this out in the open. You did a damn good job and we want you to keep it up. But you can tell Castle to go fuck himself," Lean said.

"I'll try to find some other words for it," Louisa said with a nod.

"Only if you want to," Mabry added, laughing to himself.

"No ones knows the department better than you Louisa. We're lucky to have you and we want to keep you here. We hope all of this is nothing more than a hiccup. Are we clear?" Takeda asked.

"Crystal. Sir," Louisa said as she folded up the rest of her leather attache.

Louisa rode the elevator down to the parking garage, struggling to not rip her briefcase to shreds and set fire to the building so tall above her. Somehow, she knew Bradshaw would be waiting for her.

He didn't say anything. She waited but the frustration became too much for her.

"You should be proud of yourself. You did good, showing up with 64 million dollars in the moment we needed it most. I hardly could have done better myself," Louisa said.

"I understand if you're frustrated," Bradshaw said as Louisa threw the rest of her papers and jacket into the back seat of the convertible.

"Fuck you. You could have told me. You made me look like a fool in there. I had no idea and I looked like a fucking jackass because of you," Louisa pinned the pointer finger of her left hand into Bradshaw's collar."Truce?" Bradshaw squeaked.

"Fuck you."

"I did you a favor, you know. You don't have to

admit that you needed help. Everybody will think you pulled this off on your own. Castle will get drowned out with the rest of the hanger's on and you'll come out of this looking like your plated in sterling," Bradshaw said.

"I don't need your help. Just go away. For this brief moment in time our histories are intertwined, and in a few years that will no longer be the case. After that we're done and I won't owe you a fucking thing. Are we clear?" Louisa said, leaning close to Bradshaw.

"Crystal," Bradshaw responded.

Louisa threw open the driver side door of her convertible and climbed inside. The rest of her papers filled the passenger seat. She started the engine. Bradshaw stood a few feet away in the yellow halo of parking lights.

"Fuck you," Louisa said flatly as she put the convertible in gear and pulled out of the garage back into the bright California daylight.

TWELVE

The long hallways seemed to stretch on forever and Cassie had to steady herself against the wall more than once to make it back to their room. David leaned in and offered his arm.

"No, I'm fine really," Cassie said, trying to convince herself as much as David.

As soon as the door opened, Cassie rushed to the restroom and threw up. David held her blond red hair back and stroked the back of her neck with a cold, wet washcloth. When it seemed like the worst was over, he turned and filled a glass tumbler with cold water and offered it to Cassie.

She drank thirstily, leaning up against the corner of the bathroom between the large tub and the far wall. The blue and white tiles outlined her small frail figure.

"I bet I look pretty great right now, huh?" Cassie asked with the closest to a smile she could muster.

David leaned in and kissed her forehead softly.

"You look beautiful. I'm sorry you're feeling so terrible. That's the last time we go for the special cocktails," David answered.

In a rush, the sickness hit her again. She bent over and coughed but nothing came out. There was nothing left in Cassie. David helped her up and back into the bedroom of the hotel room. He pulled the sheets back for her and helped her under the covers, pulling the thick comforter up tight around her face.

"I don't know how you aren't feeling this drunk," Cassie said, still struggling to smile.

David walked back towards the bathroom. He stood framed in the doorway of the bathroom and smiled back at her.

"Get some sleep, you'll feel better in the morning," he said.

David turned and Cassie heard the faucet of the shower turn on. A few moments later, sleep came to her.

In the back of her head, Cassie knew she was dreaming. Something was off, just slightly different than the world she knew. It was brighter, sounds and images accentuated and drawn out. It made her anxious.

A cold wind came up from the far side of the plateau. She didn't know how she had gotten there but part of Cassie felt as if she had been here all along. As if she had been born meant to die there, an inevitable goal towards which she been propelled her entire life.

A few scraggly trees stood just barely taller than Cassie. Wind ripped through them and even though they were free of leaves, their branches swayed and rattled together making a soft creaking sound with each gust. Cassie could see her cold breath in the air. She wore only a thin blue nightgown but couldn't feel the cold against her skin. The rocks were sharp and cut her feet but still she felt nothing, even when small patches of blood began to outline her last few steps.

Against the horizon, a large oak tree stood out against the dim slate sky. Cassie began to make her way towards the tree. For a long time it didn't seem to get any closer, like the earth would stretch out in front of her with each new step. Her movement taking her nowhere in particular but still leaving her right where she was. Her feet began to hurt, she could feel the frozen earth cold against her skin as it found its way into cut open flesh on the soles of her feet. Her breath fogged more against the cold air as she walked. She pulled the thin nightgown closer around her body and walked on, unsure of the reason but confident in the direction.

As she neared the tree, the sound of wind sweeping over the rocks was replaced by a new sound Cassie was surprised to realize came from the tree itself. Soon, the air filled with the soft sounds of a wind chime. The sound seemed to mean she was getting closer and Cassie hurried her pace, rushing to the tree regardless of her cut feet. Each new step left a long scarlet streak against the cold rocks. Cassie's blood the only evidence that anything human had ever found this place or would ever find it again.

When she was a hundred feet or so from the tree, Cassie stopped. A man lay beneath the tree, leaning against the large trunk. His hands stretched behind his head with one foot kicked over the other as if stretched out sunning himself along some forgotten coast. He whistled a tune Cassie remembered but couldn't quite place. The man didn't notice her. She stood alone in the open plain but still he didn't stop whistling or take any notice of the exposed young woman standing before him.

The chimes grew louder and stood out against the soft wind which rushed up from the side of the mountain. She was confused but walked forwards anyways.

As she approached the tree, Cassie noticed the chime sounds came from hundreds of bleached white bones hanging from long thin wire. Some of the bones no larger than a thimble and others as large as Cassie's thigh. The bones swung softly in the wind, gently knocking into each other and filling the air with ghastly notes. She couldn't see the skull, but assumed it hung from its own wire deep in the curled branches of the tree.

She took another few steps closer. The man stopped whistling, looked up at her, and smiled. He leaned one hand against the tree and forced himself up, grunting as if some part of his body ached and had refused what had been asked of it. He was in his sixties, maybe seventies. He was tall, most of seven feet and dressed in a black suit of coarse material. He brushed the dirt and dust off his pants and faced Cassie, the wind blowing back his long grey hair.

"Good evening," He said with a smile and a bow.

Suddenly, Cassie felt the cold. The wind ripped through her small gown and she began to shake violently from the wind and the chill. She pulled her thin arms around herself, now excruciatingly aware that her pale curves were plainly visible through the sheer nightgown.

The wind seemed to pick up and the soft rumble of bones against bones almost drowned out the clattering of Cassie's teeth against themselves as she shivered on the cold empty plain. The man took a few steps toward her. Cassie could feel his warmth. She desired it. Anything against the cold of the rocks and the wind and the bone tree. She stood there, looking up at the man. She knew there was darkness in him, a singular reason not to embrace him and seek shelter in his warmth.

"It's taken you a long time. Longer than any of us ever could have imagined," The man said. His accent was strange, more like he was from some other time than place. She couldn't remember but was sure she had heard the voice before.

The man stretched out his long hand. Cassie recoiled at first, pulling the small nightgown closer against her body and trying to look away from the man.

"It's alright. Everything is alright now," The man said to her.

He outstretched his hand and gently touched Cassie's cheek. A shiver ripped through her body and then she found warmth. His touch like a fire against the cold winds. She pressed her head into his hand, letting the strange man warm her. Like a lightning strike, as the man's fingers touched her skin, she knew him. The actor from the opera in New York. That seemed like a different life, so long ago. She looked up into the tall man's eyes and she was sure of it. He was the man that had played the devil she'd met under the stage what seemed like so long ago.

She tried to say something but her voice had left her. She was afraid but at the same time didn't want the man to pull his warm hand from her face.

"It's alright, you don't have to say anything. I'm just glad you're here," He said, his soft baritone voice combined with the sounds of bone against bone.

He pushed a strand of Cassie's blond red hair back over her ear and ran his hand down around her shoulder, just slightly under her night gown. Cassie thought that he would slip the small dress off her shoulder and leave her naked in the hard wind. He unhooked his fingers from her gown and brought his hand up around the back of her neck, through her hair and towards the back of her head. She felt his strong hands lock themselves in her thick hair and pull hard backwards, forcing her gaze up at him. She looked up, not afraid but curious of this strange man in this strange place.

"I'll never lose you again," He said.

And with that, the man kissed her. The moment seemed to stretch on forever, a long lost eternity on the strange plains of nowhere that Cassie had found herself upon. In one glorious instant she both loved and hated the man, unable to comprehend all the emotions swelling up inside her. Her feelings fought against themselves and Cassie found herself both desirous of and repulsed by his existence. Each emotion building up inside her consciousness until Cassie felt she would be ripped in two by strong and disparate factions of her own self. The cold was gone now.

The man stood up straight and let go of Cassie. Cassie felt a small sharp pain on her lip and gingerly pressed her hand to it. Her finger came back with a small scarlet drop of blood. She wiped again at the the small stream of scarlet running from her lip.

The man turned and walked back to the bone tree.

"It's a pleasure to see you again Cassie," the man said without turning back.

Cassie woke in fright. Her skin was cold and damp. She was breathing hard. The room was still dark and David slept next to her. The door was closed and although it wasn't cold in the room Cassie couldn't help but shiver. Her head still spun from the strong drink. More than anything she was thirsty. She threw the covers back and reached for one of the long, thick robes from the hotel, wrapping it close around her body as she walked towards the bathroom.

She didn't turn on the light so as not to wake David. She reached around the shelf for the glass that David had filled for her earlier. The white blue light of the full moon came in through the window closest to the mountain and it gave off just enough illumination for Cassie to see. She drank the cold clear water and felt better, the strange nightmare fading from her memory. Pieces of the dream drifted back and forth in her mind. She remembered the cold and her frozen breath standing out against the grey earth. She could almost hear something like wind chimes. Her eyes got more and more accustomed to the soft blue light and she could just make out her silhouette in the mirror.

As her head become clearer, her lip began to hurt. She lifted a hand gingerly to her mouth and winced with sharp pain, a small speck of blood on the tip of her finger.

David woke early the next day as the sunlight came creeping in through the sheer windows. He didn't turn on any lights for fear of waking Cassie and quietly crept out of bed to dress and put on his running shoes. There was just enough light in the room to see and David did a few quick stretches in the center of the room before looking at himself in the mirror. He was getting older, he knew it. What was once taut muscle had just now started to turn into the sort of paunch his father had worn.David turned and watched himself in profile, his stomach protruding just slightly. He tried to suck it in, it almost went flat against the rest of his body. He looked over at Cassie sleeping, the yellow sheets pulled up around her body. He wondered if she knew how much better she could do.

The air outside was cold, just above freezing. David took off from the large doors at the front of the hotel with a soft jog. He wasn't timing himself like he did in LA but running seemed a good way to get a better look at the grounds and see a few places Eddie hadn't thought to take them. David pulled the blue headband lower to keep his long hair out of his eyes as he ran.

His muscles fought him at first. Fought

against the cold. Fought against the thin air and the altitude. It was a beautiful morning, the sun was was coming up over the mountains to the east of the small bowl of rock.David turned onto one of the small, wooded roads that led away from the hotel. A road they hadn't taken with Eddie the other day. He

could feel his body getting used to the mountains and the cold air. His breath came easier. His muscles didn't ache quite as much. He followed the dirt road further and further up into the mountains and his mind started to clear. He picked up speed now and it felt good to exert himself. He wiped sweat from his eyes and kept running. The trees flew past him, blending together as he moved quickly through them.

The road took a sharp turn and climbed toward the summit of one of the peaks. David thought about turning back but something about the road and the cool air kept him going. The road got steeper as it wound closer to the peak. David kept running, losing a little speed in the ascent, then struggling to regain it when the road leveled out for a few hundred yards at the flat section of cut backs.

The road opened onto a large flat dirt patch at the summit. David stopped and knelt over, struggling to catch his breath. As soon as he stopped, the air got thinner and his muscles started to feel weak. He sucked down the thin air, smiling to himself and wondering how far he'd just run.

Dizzy and winded, leaning on his knees, David felt his age and failing human form catching up with him. A red flicker far in the distance caught David's attention. It came from back in the direction of the hotel. At first David didn't even register the movement, his body screaming for water and punishing him for pushing himself so hard on his way up the mountain. Again the red flicker. This time David stood up and turned to look.

The small amount of breath he had instantly left him. The hotel burned bright against the dark outline of trees and rock on the far side of the valley floor. The sun wasn't all the way up yet and the light from the fire stood out like a small star, yellow against the forest. Long sharp flames licked off the joined peaks of the hotel's roof. David started to run.

David could feel his muscles fighting him. Each step hurt as he rushed back down the mountain and towards the fire in the distance. He was going fast down the sharp incline, each step just barely controlled enough to not hurl him off the road into one of the thick tree trunks or snap his ankle on one of the smooth frost covered rocks that littered the path. Still he wasn't fast enough. The thick trees obscured the burning hotel in the distance but every few moments he could see the burning yellow flames standing out unnatural in the dim dawn.

The road curved off to the left. Without time to even realize what he was doing, David left the road behind to keep on a straight line through the forest towards the hotel. The fire was larger now. He was getting closer. The forest cleared for just a moment and David could see one of the large gables of the hotel's roof collapse in on itself as flames ate the building. A thick tongue of flame and smoke shot up where the roof had stood moments before. David ran as fast as he could, branches ripped at his shirt and his exposed skin. It didn't matter, he thought to himself. Nothing else mattered. He just had to get back to Cassie.

It was darker under the forest canopy. The thick trees blocked out most natural sunlight. David leapt and cleared a fallen tree that lay on the forest floor. He was closer now, almost back to the hotel. He hoped that Cassie was alright. Hoped she'd gotten out of the hotel. He was almost there, just a little further and he'd be back.

David could see the forest clearing a few hundred yards in front of him. He could feel his body collapsing but ran anyways. His body pushing harder than it ever had. Only a few yards further.

He saw the gully a few seconds before it was upon him. He couldn't have stopped or changed direction in those brief few moments, and almost instantly David found himself hurled through empty air. He hit the ground hard, feeling a bone in his right leg snap as he crashed onto the earth. He tumbled forward, bracing himself with his arms just barely in time to protect his head and neck as he fall hard onto the rocks.

For a moment he didn't know where he was. He looked up at the sky through the leaves. But that moment cleared and all the horror and urgency rushed back into him. He tried to get up but searing pain ripped through his leg and he collapsed back to the ground.

David looked up towards the hotel. He was close enough now to see it clearly. The Stanley stood bright white against the dark greens and grey of the mountain just as it had when he had first seen it driving in. No fire, no smoke.

Just before he passed out, David wondered if he was losing his mind.

FOURTEEN

"I found him just like this. He was laying at the base of the tree line," Eddie said as he threw open the passenger side door.

David was unconscious, laid out in the seat. Cassie touched his forehead softly and begged him to wake up.

"I thought he was dead," Eddie said, driving as quickly as he could over the frost covered road down from the mountains.

"Thanks Eddie," Cassie said.

"The hospital is about a half hour away, once I saw he was breathing I figured we should pick you up."

"What were you thinking David?" Cassie said to herself as much as anybody.

She bent over and kissed David's forehead. They didn't say anything else till they got to the hospital.

Two male nurses lifted David from the bench seat of the truck and onto a gurney. They rolled him quickly in through the side of the building directly to an operating room. Cassie followed the crowd of doctors and nurses taking measurements of David's vitals and pushing plastic I.V's into his arm. Eddie went to park the car.

At a pair of swinging doors leading into one

of the sparse operating rooms, a man stopped Cassie with an outstretched hand.

"Where are you taking him?" Cassie asked just barely able to keep back the tears that were finally finding a way out.

"Calm down. You got him here. He's going to be fine," the doctor said in a practiced, calm voice.

"I just, I don't know what happened," Cassie said.

"Thats alright, let's start with his name?" the doctor answered.

"His name's David Bannon. I'm Cassie."

"Good. Cassie, I'm Dr. Crowley and everything is going to be alright," he said and smiled at her.

The coffee was cold. It was Cassie's third cup in two hours but she sipped anyways. Eddy sat next to her, his feet propped up on one of the chairs facing them. Cassie wanted to go ask the woman at the reception desk how much longer it was going to be before she could see David but she knew the woman wouldn't have an answer.

So Cassie drank the cold coffee and sat and worried over the man she loved, confused by what strange chain of events lead the two of them to this moment.She felt her heart jump as the broad aluminum doors parted and David came out, pushed in a wheelchair by Dr. Crowley. His head was wrapped in a white bandage and his leg was covered in a thick, plaster cast. He had that dumb grin on his face. He held his arms out as if to say "I'm sorry" and Cassie started to cry.

She rushed to David and threw her arms around him, kissing him deeply. Joy and nervous excitement filled her and flowed into him through her. There was no more reason to keep the tears in so they came out, rushing in great salty gobs down her face. She turned and hugged and kissed Dr. Crowley, who was surprised and laughed.

"You big dummy," she said leaning over again to kiss David on the top of the head.

"Thank you doctor," Cassie said.

"I'm just doing my job. It looked worse than it was. He broke his leg and took a pretty bad knock to the head but he'll be fine."

"Thanks Doc," Eddy said as he held out his hand to Crowley. Eddy pulled the doctor aside a little ways down the hall and asked him a few questions softly.

Cassie took a step back and looked over David. He was a mess but she was glad he was alright.

"Do you have any idea how worried I was for you? Eddie found you laying there and thought you were dead. You know what that does to a girl?" Cassie said. The tears were finally slowing and she found herself almost laughing.

"Believe me, it wasn't on purpose. My head's still spinning," David said, forcing a smile.

"What are we going to do with you?" Cassie

asked.

"I've got no idea," David laughed back.

Cassie started pushing the wheelchair towards the front doors. Eddy finished talking to Dr. Crowley and thanked him again for his help. David waved to the doctor as Cassie pushed him through the doors.

David rode in the passenger side of the old truck with the window all the way down. Cassie sat in between the two men, David's plastered leg stretched out in front of her. An old cowboy song played on the radio. David looked out the window and in the rearview mirror watched the wheel of his wheelchair spin in the truck bed as it caught the wind going past.

After David and Cassie had thanked Eddie for driving them into town, there wasn't much conversation on the way back to the hotel. Cassie had tried to put together the story of how David had been left unconscious in the woods with a broken leg but no matter how David tried to explain it nothing really made sense.

David never once mentioned the the fire. He remembered seeing it, seeing it stand out and shoot up from the roof of the hotel as the building collapsed on itself like he was right there, watching it all happen again.

But he knew how crazy it sounded. The building was still there unharmed when they pulled up and he couldn't explain what had happened on the mountain. David looked out the window and agreed softly with Cassie when she said he needed to be more careful.

FIFTEEN

Louisa sat at her desk smoking a cigarette. The window was open and the grey smoke drifted out towards the backlot behind her. The studio hummed in the distance, lights buzzing softly, the reassuring cacophony of a thousand different worlds being photographed, packaged, and shipped to theaters around the country. Somehow it was always silent as soon as someone called "action" but those moments in between were such a mess of sound. It was almost enough to drive one mad. Louisa wondered if that is what happened to Shorter. No, he seemed to like the noise, Louisa thought to herself. Her cigarette burned down and she snuffed it out in one of Shorter's large glass ashtrays by the window.

The small speaker on her desk beeped angrily at her. It was her receptionist.

"Castle is on the other line, he wants to speak with you. He's upset," the receptionist squeaked through the speaker.

"I'm not here," Louisa said.

"Ive told him three times a day for the past week. He says that you owe him some answers. He sounds pretty angry," the girl said.

"Keep telling him I'm not here till I tell you to do something different," Louisa said frustrated.

"Yes mam, of course."

The little speaker clicked off. Louisa leaned back into her chair and stared up at the ceiling.

She still couldn't make sense of what had happened. She'd done well for herself, gaining recognition from the top brass without having to actually put anything on the line for it. But she couldn't help feel that small gnawing at the base of her spine like she'd just woke from some bad dream. Maybe she just didn't like letting Bradshaw win. It bothered her for him to know that he could do anything he wanted around here without consequence. Maybe it was just the old boys club running the show that really left a bad taste in her mouth.

The bathroom door was open and she could see the spot where she'd found her friend hanging. That didn't make her feel any better either. Regardless of how she looked at it, something was wrong, she hadn't wanted to win this way.She looked over at the pile of scripts that had been slowly growing the past couple of weeks. The board had gently indicated they wanted Louisa to find a number of pictures Worldwide could put out over the coming production season. "Safe bets" they called them. It was strange to her they were worried about safe bets but still moved ahead with pictures very nearly guaranteed to lose money. If these mystery financiers didn't care about a return, Louisa's position and skill at bringing in feature films on time and under budget suddenly became increasingly pointless. She reached over the pile of scripts and picked up another cigarette. They were going to lose a fortune with Bradshaw and nobody but me seems to give a god damned, she thought to herself.

Louisa went through the motions for the next few hours and left the studio early. Later than everyone else, but early for her. She locked her office herself with the receptionist already gone and walked to the parking lot. Pulling the big green Jaguar out of the executive lot, Louisa waved to the night patrolman and took a right instead of the left towards her apartment. She didn't know where she was headed or why she didn't go straight home but Louisa had felt a bit out of odds for the last weeks and didn't think much at all about where she was going. A drink sounded nice.

The road fell away behind the powerful car and Louisa enjoyed the warm air pulling her hair back. The yellow lights came and went in a hypnotic rhythm and without even thinking about it Louisa found herself pulling into a bar that she hadn't been to in almost 10 years. The blue and green neon sign blinked over the parking lot. The Snake Pit.

Inside, the bar was dark and sold strong drinks. Louisa had found a certain brand of happiness here when she first moved to Los Angeles after law school. She sat in a booth in the corner of the bar, she had liked that particular booth because it was dark and you could see the rest of the bar. The place hadn't changed much. A few more of the yellow lightbulbs were out. It was still early and the place was mostly empty.

One of the bartenders finished wiping a glass and made his way over to Louisa.

"Hey there, how are you?" the boy said with a southern accent that bordered on a lisp.

"Fine, how are you?" Louisa answered.

"Mighty fine. Could I get you something to drink?" The boy asked.

"Something strong with bourbon in it," Louisa answered.

"Gimme just a second," The boy said as he turned and made his way back to the bar.

Louisa took a cigarette out of her bag and lit it, looking around the bar, as much to make sure she didn't recognize anyone as out of curiosity. By the time she'd taken the first puff of her cigarette the boy returned with an amber cocktail. He placed the drink on a napkin in front of Louisa and she started counting out a few bills.

"If you promise you'll stay for a few, the first one's on the house," The boy said with a country grin.

"I think I will. Thanks," Louisa answered.

He wiped his hands on the white towel and made his way back towards his spot at the bar. Louisa eyed the boy as he walked back. She knew he wanted her. His desire was plain and simple and obvious. Part of her was even open to the idea. But her mind was unsettled. With so much happening and so little of it making sense she just wanted to be alone and to think. She smiled back when she caught him looking at her as she drank her dark, strong drink.

She'd spent a lot of time at The Snake Pit. She'd met David here. He was new to town and just starting off as a young producer, making the shift from pretty boy actor that wasn't any good to a string puller behind the curtains. She looked over at the booth where she had first met him, surprised at how smart he was for how attractive she found him. He spoke three languages and didn't smoke, which Louisa liked in a man. When she told him he was a poor actor, he said he agreed and was looking into other forms of gainful employment. She'd helped him meet people and soon it was obvious he was capable and trustworthy. He'd risen quickly.

They went home together that first night. They stayed up late smoking pot she'd bought from a one legged actor working on one of the westerns shooting on the back lot.

They'd seen each other off and on for a year or so before he came to her one day in her office and it was clear whatever might have been would never be. Louisa shook his hand when he left. She laughed to herself as she took another drink from the glass. She wondered if other women shake a man's hand when they say goodbye.

She hadn't thought about The Snake Pit for years but now she was here she could see and feel little bits of her past coming up from the pools of light above the bar and in the dark corners of the large room. The pool table where she'd won a hundred dollars from Errol Flynn two weeks before he died sat unused on the far side of the bar. Not much had changed in all the years since she'd last been there.

She lit another cigarette and motioned for the cowboy to bring another drink. He brought it over and she leaned back into the cracked leather of the booth. She thought about the time she'd sat right in that very same booth talking to a wannabe starlet from Kansas City. Louisa had asked the girl her hopes and dreams and what sort of pictures she liked to watch back in her small home town. Later that night, the girl came home with her. It was the only time Louisa had been with a woman and she hadn't much cared for it, unsure of what to do with herself and more self conscious of her body than she'd ever been with a man. The girl was beautiful and too nice for Los Angeles. She had seemed heart broken when Louisa told her she should go home and that she couldn't help her get a job. Louisa wondered what had happened to the girl. She knew the girl hadn't hit it big on the silver screen and just hoped she'd gone home. The girl deserved that much, Louisa thought to herself.

Another drink. Another cigarette.

Louisa could feel the world becoming topsy turvy around her. She walked up to the bar and placed a single large bill down on the dark stained wood. The cowboy picked up the bill and turned to make change but Louisa was already an outline in the door.

Louisa paused at the edge of The Snake Pit's parking lot. There was a slight chill to the air so she rolled the windows up and turned on the heater in the car. Old times had caught up with her. Louisa fiddled with the radio dial and thought about the disparate, intersecting lines that made up her life. An old Patsy Cline song began to play. Then Louisa noticed the red Cadillac rush past. Benson Bradshaw's bright red Cadillac.

She pulled out east onto the small road behind Bradshaw. She hit the gas and drove the opposite direction from her apartment, her office at the studio. Away from every part of her life she should be going home to. She was sure he hadn't noticed her. He weaved the car lazily through the two lanes of after dark traffic. The Jaguar could easily outpace the Cadillac but Louisa hung back, letting Bradshaw get a few streets ahead at times to make sure he didn't notice being followed.

Louisa felt a little like one of the characters from the scripts piled on her desk. Some fatally wounded character, driven by principle and an abrupt moment that changed their life forever. She wondered why all private eyes were men. The Patsy Cline song slowly found its conclusion and the disk jockey put on another. Louisa didn't recognize this one but liked the melody. The Cadillac picked up speed on one of the long straightaways coming off the freeway and headed up into the canyons. Louisa pressed down on the gas pedal and the song played on.

The streetlights no longer lit the road and Louisa hung back a half mile or so. She could see the headlights of Bradshaw's red Cadillac weaving in and out of the deep green canyons almost black in the moonless night. Each time the lights careened behind one of the curves of the canyon walls Louisa worried she would lose him and face a long drive home with plenty of time to think of how pointless this all had been. The yellow headlights never disappeared. They drove for what felt like most of an hour.

In the distance, Louisa saw the headlights of Bradshaw's car pull off the main road and stop in the darkness. The headlights raked against a large wrought iron fence set into two stone pillars. Louisa kept driving and quickly closed the gap.

"Shit, shit shit." She thought to herself.

Louisa kept driving, watching Bradshaw say something into the small intercom set into a pillar next to the stone driveway. The gates swung open and Bradshaw pulled the large red car up the massive driveway towards what Louisa could only imagine to be one of the real mansions that made the homes of Hollywood look like the cheap sets of plywood. Louisa drove on and parked the car a mile down from the gate in a soft patch of earth off the road to the left.

You're drunk. You should go home and forget this ever happened, Louisa thought to herself. She knew she wasn't going home, but still it made her feel better to think the words.

Louisa locked the car and started up the canyon road towards the house. She couldn't move too quickly because of how dark it was. She was thankful no other cars came down the road, sure they would either call the police or stop to see if she needed help.

She came to the corner of the lot. A tall fence of limestone and granite stood cutting off any view of the house from the street. She followed the wall back a little ways off the road looking for a place to climb over that wouldn't be visible from the street. Louisa slipped off her white satin heels and pulled herself up onto the granite shelf of the wall.

Her heart rate quickened and Louisa half lowered half fell over the far side of the wall onto the mansion grounds. She fell hard but the earth was soft and she didn't seem to have hurt anything. She brushed the dirt off her blouse and looked around, her eyes still struggling to adjust to the moonless night. Then Louisa realized how large the grounds were. The house was nowhere to be seen and the fence seemed to stretch to the horizon. Louisa could hardly imagine such a large property existing so close to the Los Angeles city lines.

Far off in the distance, on top of a small hill, a streetlight illuminated the spot where the driveway curved out to the left further back into the property. Louisa left her white shoes at the base of the wall, afraid of forgetting where she had climbed over, and started towards the dim light through the trees. She stayed just far enough from the driveway so that she could hide in the trees if a car came or went. No cars drove past. Louisa quickly reached the light.

She stood just at the edge of the pool of light and took her bearings. She was at a high point of the property and could now see the house further off in the large forest. She could also see the road stretching back into the canyons behind her. She paused for a moment to catch her breath then started off towards the large mansion.

After years of working for moguls and stars, Louisa was genuinely impressed and curious about such a fortune quietly hiding out here in the canyons. The building was wood, stone, and dark glass. Three faces of the building were lit up with blue tinted lights that raked up at the structure from below.

She came up through the trees towards the

face of the building with the fewest lights. She saw Bradshaw's car parked along with a few other expensive cars in the front of the house. She didn't know if they could see out from the large windows of the mansion so she did her best to stay in the shadows. Her bare feet hurt from walking on the hard earth but she kept moving around the far side of the building.

At the back of the house, a large window opened up into a huge room. She came to group of trees that stood just close enough to give her a view into the room. She hoped it was far enough away where she couldn't be seen. A group of men dressed in suites stood in the center of the room. Louisa could make out the large mess of Bradshaw's tangled hair. Once Louisa's eyes had adjusted to the light coming from the room, she noticed she recognized some of the other men standing with Bradshaw. Two of the men from the holding company that had purchased partial ownership in Worldwide years ago chatted idly with Bradshaw. Takeda, the Japanese executive she had meet when her deal with Castle had been pulled out from under her. An investment banker from New York that she'd seen at a formal event the year before. The rest of the faces were strangers. Louisa counted 9 men all together.

At the far side of the room, white medical machinery stood against large vinyl sheets hanging from hooks to create a sectioned off portion of the room which Louisa couldn't see into. The pumps and arms of the machines moved repetitively up and down in their endless tasks. Louisa wondered what was on the far side of the vinyl sheeting. Louisa moved to another group of shadows to get a better view into the room.

A tall slender woman dressed in a long black gown entered carrying tall drinks on a silver tray. She handed the drinks to each man and set the tray down on a counter. She bent and adjusted one of the machine's dials. She checked that everything was working and wrote down a few of the numbers from the readouts attached to large pumps. Seemingly satisfied, she took the last glass off the silver tray and turned to address the men. The conversation in the room ceased instantly and the men looked up at the tall beautiful woman in silence. She spoke for a few moments as if giving a toast or an introduction. The woman raised her glass and the men did the same. In silence, they all drank the dark red wine in unison. The woman collected the glasses and carried the tray off into another room, returning a few moments later. She held her arms out in front of her and motioned for the men to take seats in the chairs set up in neat rows facing the vinyl sheeting. The woman in the long dress walked up to the plastic curtains. She said a few more words and pulled the curtains back on their metallic casters. Everyone was still and silent.

Behind the white curtain, a man lay on a hospital bed dressed in dark dark robes. Wires and tubes ran in and out of his body in a dozen different places. The flesh of his arms was grey and taut around the bone and muscle of the man's form. Louisa adjusted her position to see better into the makeshift hospital room. The woman approached the old man on the large hospital bed and gently nudged his shoulder, as if waking him from a dream. The machines pumped strange liquids in and out of the old man's form.

Louisa could see the old man's hand rise from the hospital bed. It's spotted skin barely clinging to the man's thin flesh and dragging a handful of thin I.V tubes into the air along with it. As the old man moved, the men in the chairs applauded softly. The woman nodded back to them, as if telling them thank you. Louisa watched the woman lean down close to the old man's face as if he were whispering something in her ear but the vinyl sheeting blocked Louisa's view. The woman turned and recounted the man's words to the group and again the small crowd cheered. The woman leaned back down to listen to the old man again and Louisa moved to another group of trees to get a better view. The woman related the old man's words again to the group but this time one of the men sitting in the chair stood up and began to speak. In a flash, the woman was standing in front of the man and reached out and struck him hard across the face. Louisa had barely seen the woman move but the blow seemed vicious even from Louisa's vantage point in the tree line. The woman ran her hands down the sides of her tight black dress regained her composure. The man quietly took his seat.

The woman leaned back down to listen to the old man in the hospital bed and Louisa's breath left her. Where the skin and form of the man's face should have been there was only a bright red polyp of bone and tissue. Louisa was close enough to make out the tendons and muscles moving in the old man's face as he whispered into the woman's ear. Louisa fought back the impulse to vomit in the shadows of the old building.

The woman turned and raised her hand, motioning for one of the men to come to the hospital bed. Louisa was surprised to see Bradshaw stand and walk slowly toward the old man's bed side. He stopped when he reached the side of the bed, knelt down on one knee, and kissed the grey skin of the old man's hand. Bradshaw turned and leaned close to the old man's gore covered face and listened as he whispered something into Bradshaw's ear. Bradshaw faced the small crowd and recounted the words with his hands held high above him. The men stood and began to cheer.

Louisa started to run.

As the light from the building fell off behind her Louisa thought for a moment she was lost in the dark woods of the property. It was colder now and the thin blouse she wore gave no warmth. As she ran, her mind ran wild with what she had just seen.

She ran for a long time before she realized what a mistake she had made not heading back towards the long driveway that had guided her up to the house. The forest was almost completely dark without a moon in the sky and for the first time in years Louisa felt truly and deeply afraid.

She quit running and forced herself to stand still for a moment, catch her breath and figure out which way to the street and her car. She regretted every part of her night following Bradshaw and wished only that she could erase in her mind whatever had taken place in the old mansion. Louisa forced the self pity and the fear from her thoughts and walked through the nearly pitch black night with her arms wrapped tight around her.

When the wall came up from out of the darkness, Louisa almost screamed but managed to stay silent. She touched the large stone wall to make sure that it was real then turned right and only had to walk a few dozen yards before she found a place where she could reach the top of the wall. With a running start she made it up and over the cold stone wall. Louisa hoped there was nothing hiding in the dark on the other side of the fence and quickly lowered herself down and fell the rest of the way onto the cold earth. She kept the wall to her right and quickly made her way back down to the road that had led her up into the canyon. The green Jaguar was where she had left it and she could barely contain her joy as she unlocked the car and climbed inside, feeling warm and safe in the large car. She locked the door.

She put the car in gear and pulled out onto the road heading back down and out of the canyon, shooting gravel and dirt behind her as she accelerated. She could feel the blood running down the cut soles of her feet as she drove barefoot away from the hills.

SIXTEEN

David held one of the large white painkillers up between his thumb and forefingers spinning it softly around on its axis. His broken leg was propped up on one of the large velvet chairs in the main lounge of the hotel room bar."I'm not quite sure what they put in these things, but I like it," David said as he tossed the pill into his throat. Cassie handed him a drink of water.

It was a bit of a scene when they had first arrived from the hospital but most curious parties had heard the story and now David and Cassie were left to themselves. The hotel staff was incredibly helpful and Cassie was glad they were in such good hands. A chef had even come out from one of the hotel's kitchen's to see if there was anything special he could make for David.

Cassie set the glass of water down on the tray and leaned back in the large red velvet chair, staring across the low table at David. He still hadn't offered any real explanation and Cassie knew something was wrong.She tried to keep the image of Eddie lifting David's limp body out of her mind. The body of the person she loved covered in blood, limp like a rag doll. He would have died if Eddie hadn't come around. She knew that now.

But David was alive and back at the hotel and

that was all that mattered to her now. If he wants to tell me, he'll tell me, she thought to herself.

In an attempt to take both their minds off the day, Cassie had spread the portfolio of photographs and notes about the Bradshaw film out onto the dark leather coffee table between them. There hadn't been much progress in the last couple of days and David's accident wasn't going to help. Having got the developed photographs back from Cartwright, Cassie now found herself with a daunting amount of pictures to organize and sort by possible locations for different scenes in the script. This was Cassie's least favorite part of the job. All of the excitement of searching for some new place that would fill perfectly the strange ideas of someone else's story was now gone, replaced with an endless amount of organization, list making, and paper work. And her work had doubled now that David was hopped up on those painkillers. Cassie could barely stand to look at the mound of paperwork but she was relieved to have something to do besides worry.

The photographs came out pretty well. After she'd gotten them back, she and David had gone through them and made a first pass of what would make it into the film. Wide shots of the front of the hotel, some of the larger corridors, and a few of the hotel rooms. Cassie had asked Cartwright to have the photographs sent back to Louisa for approval but hadn't heard anything in a few days.

With the shock of the accident and playing nurse to David, Cassie hadn't thought about the main office in L.A for almost two days.

Now she realized how strange it was she hadn't heard from Louisa. Cassie had issues with the woman but she was prompt if nothing else. Cassie flipped through some of the photographs idly. She flipped over the photo of David and Eddy drinking those signature cocktails in the main bar of the hotel and was reminded of the awful strong drink. She lifted the picture closer to look at the funny grin David wore on his face and looked over at the sleeping man she loved sitting in the velvet chair next to her.

She smiled and idly looked back at the photograph when she noticed something strange. Although she was sure she hadn't noticed anything like it when they were drinking and making merry that night not so many days ago, Eddie's eyes appeared almost completely black in the photograph. Black and dead, void of any glint or reflection.

Cassie rubbed at the photograph with the soft corner of her yellow knit sweater, assuming that whoever ran the photography store had gotten some unknown substance on her print.

"Excuse me mam," the bellboy said, surprising Cassie with a shudder with a jolt from her chair.

"There is a phone call for you," He said with a bow. The bellboy held out his hand to Cassie leading in the direction of the hotel's small business office. The bellhop held the door for Cassie and she entered the small, copper trimmed office.

Cassie lifted the receiver to her ear.

"Hello, Cassie speaking," she said.

"Cassie, this is Louisa," The connection wasn't great but Cassie could hear the tension and urgency in Louisa's voice.

"Louisa, good to hear from you!"

"You too Cassie, I heard there was an accident. Something happened to David?"

"He fell running and broke his leg. Hurt his head too. But we're back from the hospital and everything seems to be getting better."

"That's good, I'm glad he's okay."

"Did you get the photographs I sent the other day. It's been a little crazy around here but I was worried when I didn't hear from you."

"Cassie, listen to me, it doesn't have anything to do with that. I think that you both should come back to Los Angeles as soon as you can."

"But David's hurt, I don't think you understand, he's in a wheelchair and on these really strong pills the doctor gave him. He's not supposed to move for at least another few days..."

The line cut out. Cassie waited for another moment, not believing the other end of the phone was dead. What had Louisa meant? How was she supposed to get David out of the hotel in his injured state. She could barely get him into bed without help and the prospect of a cross country road trip back to California didn't sound realistic at the moment. But something in the way Louisa sounded made Cassie worried.

"Everything alright with the call?" The bellhop asked politely as Cassie crossed the large marble floor back to the cocktail lounge.

"Just checking in with the big boss back home" Cassie answered with a forced smile.

When she got back to the table where she had left David, a waiter was dropping off two cocktails. David was awake now and grinned sheepishly as Cassie approached.

"I didn't know where you wandered off to. I got a little scared on my lonesome," David joked as she took a seat in the love seat opposite him.

"Are you sure you should be drinking with everything that has happened to you?" She said as she lifted the cocktail to her mouth.

"The doctor didn't expressly forbid it and it helps my bones fuse back together," He said as he lifted his glass in the air and clinked it softly with Cassie's.

"No over doing it," she said sternly.

"Of course," David answered.

"I just had the strangest phone call with Louisa back in Los Angeles."

"Its about time that we heard from her. Didn't we send those photographs almost a week ago?"

David asked.

"David she sounded scared on the phone" Cassie said leaning close into David speaking in a soft voice.

"What are you talking about? She sounded scared?"

"I don't know how else to describe it. She sounded frightened and told me to leave," Cassie said.

"What does that mean?" David tried to push himself up from the chair but the painkillers and cocktail had begun to work.

"I don't know. She didn't say why but that was the first thing that I was gonna ask. The line cut out."

David leaned back in the chair and fiddled nervously with the clasp of his wristwatch. Cassie drank the rest of her cocktail hoping it would help. Cassie could feel it coming and was helpless to stop it. The wave of exhaustion hit her all at once. The worry and the fear crashed over her like a cold wave.

"I don't know what happened to you out there. I have no idea what this woman is talking about. I just feel like we're alone out here in the middle of nowhere. I don't even know what I'm doing anymore," Cassie started to trail off.

David leaned up in his chair and reached out to take Cassie's hand. Her hand was hot in his and he found a comfort in the touch, maybe even more so than Cassie who finished her speech and looked up at David with her large eyes that begged him to promise everything was going to be alright. David saw the cost the last few days had taken upon Cassie. She'd done so well to hold it in until just that moment. He finally realized how much she had held him up at her own expense. Not talking about what had happened out there in the forest. Unsure if what he had seen was real. Unable to say with any real certainty that he was not insane. His own confusion had hurt Cassie more than even himself.

"Cassie. I'm sorry," David said.

She leaned close to him and kissed him on the cheeks and on the head and all over his face. The tears came freely now from Cassie's eyes, unafraid of letting the last of her fear show. She sat in his lap. He let out a quick shout of pain as the pressure of her weight hit the cast over his broken leg. She repositioned herself and fell softly into his arms. She was happy to be comforted and tried to comfort him in return.

"It's alright, everything is alright," David found himself saying even though he didn't know if he believed it. Cassie buried her face between his shoulder and neck. David could feel it was about time for another of the white pills.

David didn't know why he didn't tell Cassie what he had seen out in the forest as she lay in his arms and wept. Maybe it would have made everything better. Maybe they would have left that night if he was honest with her about what he'd seen.

But instead David held her and he comforted her and he waited for her to quit crying in part just so he wouldn't cry himself. David shivered with a cold sort of feeling he hadn't been able to get off the back of his spine since the accident.

SEVENTEEN

The hotel was kind enough to switch David and Cassie to a room on the ground floor. It made things easier for David in the wheelchair. Cassie held the door to the room open and David did his best to roll the chair in on his own. His strength hadn't quite come back and the pills he was taking every couple of hours didn't help. He struggled a few feet into the room and Cassie rushed forward and caught him, putting his arm over her shoulder. She pushed David onto the side of the bed and picked up the heavy plaster cast to help him lift it onto the foot of the bed. He reached up and put his hand on the small curve of her waist.

"Thank you," He said.

"For what?" She asked as she fussed with a cushion to put under the heel of his cast.

She leaned over and kissed him deeply.

From the soft repetition of her breath, David knew she was asleep and he struggled to get out of bed without waking her. It was the middle of the night. The hotel was silent, as if they were the only people in it. Most of the other patrons seemed to reside in other parts of the hotel.He gingerly lifted his cast foot out of bed and swung it down to the floor. He took the two crutches from the side of the bed and did his best to silently make it to the restroom.

David opened the medicine cabinet and fumbled with the two or three pill bottles Cassie had put up in the shelves behind the mirror. The light to the bathroom was off and in the dim grey David couldn't tell the bottles apart from each other. He squinted and struggled with the bottle he figured would be a good option. The bottle came open with a soft pop and David poured one of the pills out into his hand. His leg throbbed gently at his side but he drank another glass of water to wash down the painkiller and told himself the feeling would stop once the medicine kicked in. David fumbled for his crutches in the dark bathroom before finding them and starting back for the bed. The room was cold, as if someone had left a window opened.He sat down gently on the side of the bed and tried to itch a spot under the cast. He couldn't reach it with his fingers so he looked around on the bedside table for something to dig a little deeper under the plaster. He scratched again at his leg and waited for the painkiller to kick in.

The flicker of shadow beneath the door caught David's eye. He almost forgot the shadow as soon as it was gone and went back to looking for something to scratch the inside of his cast when the shadow returned. This time he froze and watched as the silhouette of two feet stopped just outside his door outlined by the light still on in the hallway. David sat on the foot of the bed in total silence, waiting. For a long moment nothing happened. David wondered if he was dreaming.

David looked over at Cassie, her breath slowly rose and settled in her chest. David was glad Cassie wasn't awake. He felt the muscles in his chest and back contract as the room got colder. David hadn't felt this way in long time and couldn't quite place the sensation. Soon he realized the feeling was terror.

One of the crutches leaned against the bed. He placed it under his shoulder as quietly as he could. Still unsure if his mind was playing tricks with itself, the shadow at the base of the door shifted and David heard the quiet jingle of keys. David was standing now, moving as silently as he could towards the door. The painkiller was kicking in now. His head getting lighter, he could feel the blood in his veins thinning out. The itch was gone, replaced with the strange tingling fear of someone standing outside the door to his hotel room in the dark quiet night.

He crutched another couple feet towards the door and stopped to listen carefully in the dark room. David leaned close to the door, he could almost reach out and touch it. He took another step, making sure he didn't make a sound. He put the weight on his good foot and leaned closer to the door, struggling to hear anything in the hall. He looked down. The shadow was still there, just on the other side of the door.

David's foot started to hurt. He hadn't stood this long since the hospital and David wasn't sure how much longer he could keep it up. He tried to switch the crutch to the other side of his body, but he lost his balance and had to catch himself on the door frame with a soft thud. The shadow under the door turned and walked away down the hall.David reached out carefully and unlocked the door. The key clicked softly into place as the latch retracted into itself. David stood there, breathing heavily as he waited to open the door.He took a deep breath and steeled himself for whatever waited outside in the hallway. He leaned the crutch against one of the high backed chairs on the hotel room. David took in a deep breath and steeled himself to open the door. The door rocked back, almost ripped from its hinges. He fell backwards, just barely catching himself on the side of the bed. Cassie woke screaming. And just as suddenly as the noise had come, it was gone again. David and Cassie sat in silence both scared and breathing hard.

"David?" Cassie asked.

"Everything is alright. Everything is going to be alright," David answered.

"What was that?" Cassie asked.

"There was someone outside," David said, struggling to get himself back to his feet.

In a flash he was at the door and turned on the light. He held his crutch in front of him like a weapon, struggling to keep his balance on one foot but determined and headstrong regardless.

"Get behind me," David said. He reached his hand out to open the door.

"David don't!" Cassie screamed.

No one was there. David cautiously poked his head out of the door, the corridor empty in both directions all the way down the long hall leading to the front of the hotel.

"What was that? I wake up and you're laying on the the ground shouting. Don't treat me like I'm some fucking kid. What was it David? What the hell is going on?" Cassie shouted.

"Somebody was out here. But they're gone now, we're going to be fine. I promise you everything will be alright," David answered.

EIGHTEEN

The roads up the mountain had been iced over for weeks. Louisa fought to keep the car on the road and had already pulled over twice to scrape the icy snow from the windshield. The white truck she had rented at the airport came with a set of chains but it had taken Louisa most of an hour to figure out how to put them on. She cursed quietly as she turned the knob on the dash in a vain effort to defrost the wind shield.

It had been two and a half months since David and Cassie had disappeared. When they didn't call or come home, Louisa had called the police in both Colorado and California. She'd even hired a private investigator to try and find the young couple. Everyone had been kind and gracious and helpful but of no help. She had found herself on a plane to the Donan Hotel ten weeks later.

She wondered if she would still be the head of production at the studio when she got back. It didn't really matter to her anymore.

She was no longer involved in the Bradshaw film but she had managed to look at one of the file folders she had her assistant borrow from the copy room. The film was set to start shooting in the coming weeks but nobody from the production would be at the hotel yet. Most people thought that David and Cassie had just run off to get married and would reappear with wild tales and suntans. Louisa thought it ridiculous of Bradshaw to keep moving forward with the hotel David and Cassie had found with the young couple still missing.

She gripped the steering wheel tighter as she heard a clap of thunder in the distance. The road carved off towards the right, Louisa hoped she was almost to the Donan and looked forward to getting off the road. As she came around the peak of the mountain a large flat clearing opened up and she could see The Donan dug into the base of the mountain. She fumbled with the pile of photographs sitting in the passenger seat.

Louisa didn't stop but knew this was the exact same spot where Cassie had taken that first photograph of the hotel so many weeks before. She must have looked at that photo a couple of thousand times.

Louisa shivered and exhaled her hot breath into the palms of her hands. The steering wheel felt frozen solid. She hit the control panel in the center dash, trying to get the heat to blow a little hotter. She missed her convertible. The heat still didn't turn on and having crested the grey peaks of the looming mountains Louisa started the long drive down the other side towards the hotel. It was even slower going down.

Her heart beat a little faster as she pulled

up under the large eave of the Donan. In the days following the young couple's disappearance, Louisa was pulled from the Bradshaw film and she could tell her status at Worldwide had changed for the worse. The police had sent investigators out to the hotel with photographs of David and Cassie but came up with nothing. The investigator Louisa hired herself said the staff of the hotel were friendly and helpful and remembered the young couple had stayed in the hotel for a week or so sometime ago but had records clearly showing the couple to have checked out of the hotel the day after Louisa had spoken to Cassie on the phone. After that, their trail went cold.

The police helping Louisa in Colorado had even gone through the car crashes on record for the two weeks following Louisa's phone call with Cassie. She didn't want to think of it but now that she found herself at the wheel of a 4x4 truck alone in the snowy mountains, she was ready to admit the possibility that their car had tumbled off the edge of one of these mountain roads and they had been lost to the wilds of the mountain. Louisa almost wished that was the truth although somewhere deep down she knew it false.

When she opened the door the cold air hit her hard and sucked the breath out of her chest.

Louisa took her only bag out of the passenger seat and started towards the large glass door at the front of the hotel. Cartwright rushed to her to give her a hand with her luggage but she motioned that she was fine carrying it herself.

"Welcome to The Donan," he said as he pulled the large copper door open for her.

"Thank you. Do you have somewhere to park that thing?" she said.

"Yes mam," he answered. She handed him the keys to the rented truck and watched as he turned and started the small car and pulled out into the road leading to the back of the hotel. It was snowing harder now, and Louisa was glad she'd made it down from the white peaks before the storm got any worse.

The inside of the hotel was warm and Louisa was surprised to find she felt comfortable in the hotel. She took a few steps into the large lobby and stomped the snow off her boots in one of the large mud catches beneath the windows. Louisa unwrapped her scarf and placed her wallet down on the counter beside her.

"My name is Louisa McKay. We spoke on the phone," she said, struggling to keep her teeth from chattering as she got used to the warmth inside the hotel.

"Of course, Ms. McKay. What a pleasure it is to finally meet you. Have the authorities had any luck in finding your friends?" Cartwright answered.

"If they had do you think I'd be here? Look, I don't want to be here. I want to believe you when you say they aren't here. But something kept catching in the back of my throat every time I'd say I felt alright about everything. So now I'm here. I've been driving through a snow storm most of the day. I'm tired and I'm pissed off so please cut the shit and show me to my room."

Cartwright stood still a moment, unsure of what to do. Gears spun slowly against themselves behind the glistening eyes with which he watched Louisa. Her curtness visibly upset him for a split second causing his polite expression to slip. And then just as quickly, a smile crept back upon his face.

"Of course madame. Right this way," Cartwright said and turned to lead Louisa towards her room.

The hallway was surprisingly large but warm and Louisa was glad they didn't have too far to go. There seemed to be no other guests at the hotel and Louisa was glad to have a room on the ground floor.

"Thank you," Louisa said when they reached the front door of her room.

"Feel free to ring if you need anything. Night or day, it makes no difference," Cartwright said before starting back down the long hallway.

Louisa took a few steps into her hotel room and placed her bag at the foot of the bed. She stood for a moment, then turned and stepped back into the hall. Cartwright was already a few dozen yards away, moving down the long hallway slowly even for a man of his age.

"Mr. Cartwright, I apologize if I was short with you," Louisa said.

Cartwright turned and she could see his body straighten for a moment, as if in thought, before he smiled back at Louisa.

"That's quite alright Madame," he answered.

Louisa shut the door behind her. She closed her eyes and breathed deeply. Louisa had never enjoyed travel and would have preferred to be alone in her apartment. Her head ached and for a moment Louisa thought she was having one of the migraines that had started happening more and more recently. But the wave of anxiety and shortness of breath quickly passed and Louisa opened her eyes again to find herself in the large and comfortable hotel room.

Louisa turned the tap to run a hot bath and went back into the bedroom. She took her clothes off and lay them neatly on the bed. She wrapped herself in a large towel she found in the bathroom and waited for the tub to fill. When steam from the hot water filled the small bathroom she unwrapped the towel and slid gently into the water. After the long drive in the frozen car the hot water jolted her body back into itself.

She lay back with her head on the porcelain tiles of the tub and closed her eyes, feeling at ease for the first time in days. She was tired. Louisa knew she worked too much. She could feel the years catching up with her. She could see the days dragging their costs from her body. For the first time in her life Louisa felt old.

"What the fuck are you doing?" Louisa said aloud and dipped her head under the hot water.

The next morning, Louisa woke early and looked through the photographs and documents Cassie and David had sent from their time at the hotel. There wasn't much, maybe 30 or 40 photographs and a few pages of location reports. Still, Louisa searched for a starting point.

There was a small kettle in the room and she made herself a cup of tea and sat in the window nook flipping through the photographs. Cassie had been a good photographer and plenty of the photo's were of David, hitting a sensitive nerve with Louisa as she flipped through the couple's travelogue moments. She liked the photos when David seemed surprised, those little moments where Cassie had snuck up and clicked the shutter quietly without his knowing.

She stopped and held one of the prints up to the light coming in from the window. The blue grey sunrise was bouncing off the snow on the mountains outside and giving just enough light for Louisa to make out details in the image. David was laughing while he filled up the tank of gas. He was turning back towards the camera. The edges of the photo was blurred by the world moving too fast for Cassie to capture and hold on too. He looked happy, Louisa thought to herself. Louisa wondered if he was ever that happy with her. She put the photograph back into the large folder.She took a few more drinks of tea and started to get dressed. Snow fell outside the window, building up against the rest that had come down as she slept. The view outside looks like something out of the movies, Louisa thought to herself.

"I want to see where David got hurt," Louisa said before she'd even made it all the way to the front desk.

"Of course. And how did you sleep last night?" he asked as he finished organizing the paperwork he was pushing back and forth on the desk and turned to face Louisa, not at all surprised by the request.

"Fine, thank you. I'd like to see where it happened, as soon as possible if that is agreeable with you," Louisa said sternly.

"Of course," The man turned and lifted the phone receiver off its cradle and asked someone on the other end of the line to rush to the front lobby as quickly as possible.

"Our groundskeeper will be here shortly. I suggest you eat something, breakfast will be served in just a few moments," The man said with a smile.

"No thank you. I'm fine," Louisa said.

A few moments later Eddie Cannahan walked in through the front door dressed in warm winter gear and a rubber parka. He took a few steps into the lobby of the hotel and stopped to brush the snow from his large frame. Cartwright made a fuss about the mess but Eddie didn't seem to care.

"I'm Eddie, I was the one that found him, found David I mean," Eddie held out his hand in greeting and smiled his broad, gap toothed smile out at Louisa.

"I'm Louisa McKay, I worked with David and Cassie," she answered.

"And you're out here looking for em?" he asked.

"Yes I am," Louisa said.

Eddie turned and started to wrap himself back up in his great, rubber parka to ward off the snow storm picking up outside. Louisa wrapped her thin jacket around her frame and started towards the door.

"Is that all you brought?" Eddie asked.

"I'll be fine."

"No, you won't. Bring one of the coats out of the back. And a thick scarf. The woman's likely to freeze to death going out dressed like that," Eddie barked.Louisa was happy the heating in Eddie's truck worked better than hers as she bounced along almost peacefully in the passenger seat. The coat was much too large but it was warm and she thanked him again for insisting she wear it. She pulled at the scarf, hot in the small cabin of the truck.

"I wanted to thank you for helping David and Cassie. When I spoke to her on the phone last, she said that someone here had driven them into town in a truck. I assume that was you?" Louisa asked.

"It was." Eddie answered.

The truck petered on towards the edge of the tree line. The snow was built up by the ploughs on the sides of the road and through the passenger window the world appeared frosted in white glass.

"Thank you."I was just doing what I ought to do."

"Do you have any idea what David was doing out there?" Louisa asked.

"Well, I just found him laying there. For a split second I thought that he was dead. But no, I can't give you any good reason that he would have ended up like that. It was just about the strangest thing I've ever seen," Eddie answered.

Eddie parked the car a little off the road in one of the only clear and level patches of ground. They climbed out of the cab and Eddie pointed east towards a group of trees coming down from the steep side of the mountains.

"It's right over here," Eddie said and turned to start walking towards the tree line.

After a couple minutes of walking through knee deep snow, they stopped at the spot where Eddie had found David. Louisa could feel her body covered in sweat under the thick clothes Eddie had given her and she was a bit lightheaded.

Louisa assumed it was from the altitude.

"I found him right here. His leg was broke," Eddie said pointing to a patch of snow.

"He must have fallen off the ridge up there and knocked himself out something bad when he hit the ground."

Louisa looked up at the rock outcropping above her. It was about 15 feet above her and if David had fallen from there he was lucky to have only broken a leg. Louisa loosened the large scarf pulled tight around her neck and started to walk up to the rocks above.

"Where are you going?" Eddie asked.

"I just want to go up and have a look. I don't know, I've never done this before," she answered. They crested the peak of the small ledge and Louisa realized she wouldn't find anything up here. She had no idea what she was looking for. Maybe David and Cassie really were just gone. It was getting colder and the snow came down more and more.

They rode back in the pickup truck with the heater working as hard as it could. Louisa held her hands together and blew into them to warm up. The truck threw snow up into the air behind it and Eddie drove slowly.

"They were friends of yours, huh?" Eddie asked.

"We worked together but yeah, we were friends," Louisa answered.

"I'm sure sorry they're gone. I wish I could help more," Eddie answered.

They parked in front of the hotel just a little off to the side and Eddie climbed out to open the door for Louisa.

"It's really coming down out there now. Usually when it gets this bad they have to close the roads back to town," Eddie mostly shouted over the wind coming down off the mountain.

"How long does it usually snow like this?" Louisa asked as they entered the lobby of the hotel.

"Hard to say. Could stop tomorrow morning, could stop a few weeks from now," Eddie answered.

They took turns brushing the snow from their shoulders and hair. Louisa took the coat and scarf and returned it to the front desk.

"I'm also the bartender. I could whip you up something to take the chill from your bones," Eddie said with a smile.

Louisa sat at the large, polished bar sipping at a freshly steaming hot toddy. The brown liquid came steaming up from the old tea cup and Louisa held it up before her face to let the steam thaw her nose and cheeks. She sat across from the window, and watched a sheet of the bright white snow come down outside the large floor to ceiling window. The small peaks of green were eclipsed outside by the white curtain of snow that hung just on the other side of the window. The drink was still too hot but she tried anyways and burned her tongue.

She set the drink down on the dark wood bar and unwrapped the brown twine that held closed the folder of Cassie's photographs.

Louisa spread the photographs out on the bar in front of her. She always did it in the same order, starting with the last roll that Cassie had sent back to Los Angeles. The first photo was from the road up in the mountains, taken just as they were cresting the peak of the mountain southeast of the hotel and saw the hotel for the first time. Louisa laid the rest out in a neat rectangle. The drink was cooler now and she took a sip as she sat there looking at the photographs, waiting to see something that she had missed. Knowing it wasn't there.

Light shot between a pair of large trees just before the road turned up towards the far mountain. Louisa turned unsure if she had been imagining something out there in the snowfall beyond the window. A few moments later, a large old Packard came bulling out from the solid sheet of white outside. The headlights cut through the snowfall as the car followed what was left of the road leading to the hotel. The large car skidded on the snow as it turned off the main road and pulled up beneath the large awning.

Louisa turned back to the photographs and looked at one of Cassie standing in the forest, atop the thick trunk of a large tree that had fallen. The concierge rang the small bell at the table next to him and the bellboy came out from his secret perch in the back room. Louisa couldn't make out what the concierge whispered to the bellboy as he ran to the coat rack to put on the thick rubber goulashes that had been drying upside down behind the desk.

The steam was still coming from the teacup in her hands and Louisa watched as the bellboy and the driver struggled to unload something from the large back door of the Packard. A tall figure was overseeing the operation and Louisa was glad that she didn't have to be out in the snow.

Cartwright held the door open long enough for a large burst of snow to come rushing in and chill the front of the hotel. Louisa watched from the bar as an old man was pushed into the Donan Hotel on a wheelchair covered in blankets. He seemed just barely conscious. A few moments later a tall, elegant woman dressed in dark fur which came up high around her neck entered the hotel. She supervised the struggling bellboy as he pushed a cart full of expensive leather luggage in from the blizzard that fell outside.

The woman was much younger than the man in the wheelchair and although the thick fur concealed the woman's form, Louisa could tell she was a tall and strikingly beautiful creature. Louisa sipped her tea and looked through one of the location reports filled out in Cassie's handwriting. Eddie went outside and started the great blue

Packard with a loud start and pulled it over to the side of the hotel somewhere.

Louisa looked up from the production report recommending the use of particular hotel rooms for particular scenes in the film just as the old man was wheeled through the large entry hall and down one of the large wings of the hotel leading off to the east. The tall woman walked a few feet behind him, unbuttoning the fox tail wrap that covered her face. She propped the fur in the crock of her arm and looked over at Louisa with a slight nod. That's all that it was, the briefest of passing moments between strangers.The world snapped into perfect focus in the small space behind the back of her green eyes as Louisa recognized the woman from the mansion in the hills. She was here at the hotel now, she'd come through a blizzard to get here. Still none of it made sense, just loose pieces butting up against each other in no clear order or pattern. She couldn't help but think of the old man in the hospital bed that night, laying there, his lips moving and the muscles and sinew of his face rippling bare and glistening with a wet shine.

The teacup shattered when it hit the floor, causing everyone within ear shot to stop what they were doing and look up at Louisa. The woman turned and stared straight into Louisa's eyes. For a moment the rest of the hotel died out in Louisa's perception and she was alone."Are you alright Miss

McKay?" Eddie asked, snapping her back into the real world.

"Oh, Oh yes. I'm quite sorry about that," Louisa said, flustered as she quickly piled the photographs and papers back into the attache and pulled the cord tight around them.

"It slipped out of my hand."

"No bother, we've got plenty. They aren't as old as they look," Eddie said with a wink.

The woman turned and lightly barked a few more orders to the bellboy pushing the wheelchair. They disappeared down one of the long hallways leading into the hotel.

"Please just put it on my room, I'm afraid I'm not feeling very well," Louisa said as she got up and turned to return to her room.

"Sure thing Ms. McKay," Eddie said as he swept up the shattered porcelain laying in front of the bar.

Louisa packed as quickly as she could. The snow continued to fall outside. She could hear the rafters of the old hotel creaking just slightly as they bent and moved under the weight of the snow falling on the roof. She threw her few possessions into the brown leather bag along with the attache with Cassie's photographs.

When she was done packing and fully dressed, Louisa paused, her head leaning against the thick oak door. She started to cry, not for any specific reason but knowing in her heart that she was a coward and that she would leave without finding her friends. Looking into the eyes of that woman in the fur coat, Louisa understood what a small role she had played in this story. A bit player filling out little sections of plot here and there. She was no hero and she never would be. She had quivered in her bones when that woman had looked her in the eyes, and in that instant Louisa understood what it was to be afraid. She didn't know, or need to understand what it was that she ran from. Louisa cried. For the first time in her life, in the face of a world she didn't understand Louisa knew what it was to feel powerless.

She stood there for a long moment with tears coming down her cheeks. She let them come and was glad they finally had found her. The comfort in admitting her helplessness slowly took over in her mind and after a few moments she stopped crying and found herself simply standing there. Perhaps she was simply out of tears, or maybe she had grown past that feeling of powerlessness upon having embraced it and let it wash over her. Either way, Louisa picked up her bag and stepped out into the hall.

The white sheets of snow outside were nearly solid and a soft whistle of the wind came through the long empty corridors of the hotel. She had the other key to the pickup truck parked up behind the hotel and didn't stop at the front desk.

"Evening Ms. McKay," Eddie said as he saw

her coming toward the large glass doors at the front of the hotel.

"Evening Eddie," She said.

She could tell he recognized she was carrying her coat and wrapped in her warmest clothing. An expression shifted in him and Louisa pressed on toward the door.

"You're not going out there with the snow coming down like it is? Are you?" Eddie asked, stepping towards her.

"Yes I am Eddie. Get out of my way," Louisa said as she stepped past the large man and opened the door.

"Ms. McKay please. I don't think you know what you're doing," Eddie pleaded with her.

The cold hit her a moment after she was outside. The snow was coming down hard. Eddie followed her outside. He took hold of her arm and stopped her.

"What are you thinking? There's no way over the mountains when it's like this," Eddie shouted, raising his voice over the wind whipping through the columns of the large overhang.

"Let go of me. I'm leaving right now," Louisa answered.

"The roads are slicked over for 30 miles in every direction. Nothing can get up here and nothing can get down. Just go back inside wait it out. The storm will clear. It'll clear, I swear," Eddie shouted.

"I'm not waiting," Louisa said, turning and walking out into the storm towards the parking lot at the side of the hotel.

"You can't make it. The roads are gone. Look around you! Don't be stupid!" Eddie called after Louisa. But it did no good for she was already gone.

The heater in the truck still didn't work. Louisa drove with the thick coat and scarf on but neither cut at the stinging cold that seeped into the cab of the small tin truck.

She hit the heater again, hoping this time would make a difference. Still nothing. The windshield wipers fought hard back and forth against the thick snow coming down outside, but they did little. She wiped at the glass on the inside trying to clear a visible patch through the frozen glass but it made little difference and she had no choice but to drive slowly on through the white walled storm outside.

She drove east, every once in a while noticing landmarks from the ride with Eddie out to the place where David had been hurt. The road peeled off to the left leading up into the mountains and back toward town. She started up the long path out of the valley. Louisa could barely see out of the window, the snow came down in an almost solid sheet now that fell as one substance instead of any smaller parts or pieces. In brief moments when the wind would change, Louisa could see the tall green spires of trees coming up around her, the void in their peaks indicating if the road veered to the right or the left as it cut its way back and forth up the grey side of the mountain.

The truck puttered and climbed up the thin road the best it could, Louisa struggling to hold the frozen steering wheel straight as the road twined back and forth, always climbing towards that sharp black peak that stood out through the white curtain.

Louisa brushed at the windshield again, wiping frost off the glass and making the frozen world outside only that much more obscured. She kept driving, knowing that if she stopped the car would never start again. She was afraid of sliding back down the mountain towards whatever waited back at its base, trapped till the storm passed. As she neared the peak, the trees grew smaller and the wind blew fiercer. The snow came down like a white ghost ripping its way over and past the truck and out into the open air thousands of feet above the valley floor.

The road turned at a sharp angle and Louisa pulled the truck towards it, guiding the old machine up onto more solid ground while gaining altitude towards the peak of the mountain. On her right, the world fell away in the distance out of the window. She was high up in the mountain now, the snow still falling with more intensity than Louisa had thought possible. She looked over the side of the narrow road, at the vastness of the chasm below. She pulled the steering wheel as far to the right as she could, hugging the rock wall of the road. In the distance she could see the road wrapping back in on itself leading up to the crest of the mountain.

Louisa pulled the steering wheel back to left around the curve and felt the tires lose purchase in the snow against the hard black rock. It was slow, as if the world was moving in microscopic increments, leading towards some inevitable goal down deep below in the shadows of the mountain. She pulled and pulled at the steering wheel of the truck. The wheels had no purchase as she slid closer and closer towards the edge of the road.

The truck stopped just a few feet short of the edge. The chain covered tires found hold and the truck held its ground there on the icy peak of the mountain.

Louisa screamed. A sharp, high pitched scream of frustration and anger and fear. When the note fell silent she put the truck back into gear and pulled the steering wheel towards the peak of the mountain.

The tires bit into the soft snow at last and the truck climbed towards its goal. The mountain fell away around her and Louisa was certain she was nearing the crest of the road leading out of the fear and darkness she had found at The Donan. The road went on for another thirty or forty feet in front of her and then she would be safe. She would be on the other side, heading back to the life she had left behind and doing her best to forget these last few months.

The yellow glow caught Louisa's eye first. It was small and just barely visible through the bright white curtains of the snow storm. But she was sure she had seen it and turned to look. Slowly, the immense fire registered in her consciousness.

The truck came to a stop and she turned to look out into the darkness and the storm and the frozen white world. The red orange flames of a great fire licked up around what was left of the Donan.

The truck stood there, just a few yards shy of the last cutback leading away from the ghastly valley. Louisa reached over to wipe at the frozen windshield with the soft sleeve of her sweater. The fire burned bright against the stark white of the snow storm coming down around it. Flames came up around the steeples of the dining room and central corridor and Louisa watched as portions of the roof fell in on themselves causing great fingers of flame to stretch up into the dark sky.

Louisa put the truck in gear and pressed softly on the gas, climbing towards that last precipice dividing her from a world she understood. The tires spun once in place and eventually bit, then suddenly ceased to grip against the feet of snow piled high against the black smooth rock of the mountain. Louisa could feel the truck start sliding but was helpless to do anything. She hit the gas and the tires spun faster and harder in place, finding nothing to grip in the soft snowfall that now covered the road. The more she spun the steering wheel or tried to gun the small transmission of the truck, the less control of the vehicle she had. Slowly the truck moved closer toward the edge of the narrow cutback.

The snow still came down hard outside. The bright yellow flames of the Donan cut against the side of the mountain. Louisa screamed as the truck edged over the side.

The truck came down end over end, twisting and crumpling in on itself as it tumbled. Finally, the truck caught between two large trees at the base of the mountain. The engine gushed gasoline and the frame was twisted so as to be unrecognizable.

Louisa's seatbelt held her in place during the never ending fall. And in some strange twist of fate, Louisa held to life, grasping at the buckle holding her in place.

The leather attache had opened during the fall down the mountain and Cassie's photographs were scattered around the cab. Louisa hung upside down from her seatbelt in the crumpled cab of the truck. She looked up at the photograph of David and Cassie in front of the Donan hotel as the snow fell.